MIDLANDS

Edited by Lynsey Hawkins

First published in Great Britain in 2003 by
YOUNG WRITERS
Remus House,
Coltsfoot Drive,
Peterborough, PE2 9JX
Telephone (01733) 890066

SB ISBN 1 84460 267 2

FOREWORD

This year, Young Writers proudly presents a showcase of the best short stories and creative writing from today's up-and-coming writers.

We set the challenge of writing for one of our four themes - 'General Short Stories', 'Ghost Stories', 'Tales With A Twist' and 'A Day In The Life Of . . .'. The effort and imagination expressed by each individual writer was more than impressive and made selecting entries an enjoyable, yet demanding, task.

What's The Story? Midlands is a collection that we feel you are sure to enjoy - featuring the very best young authors of the future. Their hard work and enthusiasm clearly shines within these pages, highlighting the achievement each story represents.

We hope you are as pleased with the final selection as we are and that you will continue to enjoy this special collection for many years to come.

CONTENTS

Poppy Durnall	34
Erika Peake	35
Kirstie Pritchard	36
Danielle Groves	37
James Fiddler	38
Jessica Lovett	39
Christopher Parry	40
Martin Pearce	41

Fairfield Prep School

Rosie Evans	42
Rahul Ghelani	43
Charlotte Boland	44
Beatrice Cooper	45
Hannah Paisley	46
Nathalie Matthews	47
Hannah Benussi	48
Charlie Richardson	49
Katarina Jackson	50
Sam Bowden	51
Edward Hayter	52
Alex Zaman	53
Harry Graham	54
Veronica Heney	55
Sarina Jassal	56
Jaysel Mistry	57
Francesca Onesti	58
Saskia Proffitt	59
Annie Stanford	60
Becky Steele	61
Emma Woods	62
Catriona Davey	63
Rebecca Holmes	64
Dharmist Bathia	65
Matthew Hargrave	66
Sophie Stevens	67
Sonia Varia	68
Ben Addison	69

John Portsmouth	70
James Ang	71
Karan Bhardwaj	72
Jessica Aryeetey	73
Charlotte Aspinall	74
Saira Badiani	75
Hannah Baxter	76
William Bourne	77
Nayan Chauhan	78
Georgina Armour	79

Greenfields Primary School

Mathew Davies	80
Ella Preece	81
Emily Smith	82
Bethany de Max	84
Sarah Pryce	85
Amy Kennelly	86
George Dourish	87
Rhian Jones	88
Jiyan Kutlay	90
Lily Jones	91

Humberstone Junior School

Debbie Reeve	92
Aimee Thompson	93
Chay Carter	94
Lauren Rees	95
Jamie McPhee	96
Sophie Greenwood	97
Matthew Smith	98
Victoria Lee	99
Hardeep Rai	100
Bilkis Ebrahim Patel	101
Anjali Patel	102
Adella Mulla	103
Leah Griffin	104
Lucy Gamble	105

The Stories

THE POND MONSTER

A loud rumbling roll of thunder echoed into the night outside as Johnny stuffed his face full of popcorn. 'Harry, Harry!' he whined. 'Where's the sugar?'

'In the cupboard,' answered Harry.

A loud thud from the living room told Harry that his best friend had just rolled off the sofa! Another rumble rattled the windowpanes then, from nowhere, a crack of golden whip, followed by a . . . power cut.

'Arrghh!' whimpered Johnny. 'Harry, I'm really scared - of the *dark!*'

Having nothing to do, the two boys finally fell asleep on the sofa, snoring.

A few days after the stormy night, Harry had been playing in the garden, alone, when bubbles began to emerge on the pond, like hot, boiling water in a pot. Next, from the murky depths below, a huge, green head. Then fangs, long and sharp, like daggers as big as elephant tusks. An icy wind clambered down Harry's spine.

When the creature's whole body appeared, Harry was fumbling to open the back door. *Safe inside*, he thought, but the pond monster squeezed in through the door, so Harry ran.

Minutes later, he had locked himself securely in the bathroom closet. Without warning, loud bangs and crashes could be heard then . . . silence.

The next few days Harry managed to persuade his parents to get rid of the pond. It took a lot of hard work but eventually they all managed to fill it in.

That evening, something amazing was on the news - a 'water monster' had been sighted in Australia. Wonder where it came from?

Amy Colburn (11)
Castlefields Primary School

THE GIRL

Rap, rap, rap. Pamela peered through the keyhole. A poor beggar girl knelt outside, seeking shelter. Pamela creaked the door open and the girl stepped inside.

Next morning, the girl's eyelids flickered open in time to follow the fuzzy shape of Pamela towards the curtains. '*No!*'
Pamela spun around.
'Don't open them! I . . . have a headache!'
Pamela nodded graciously. 'Very well. I've found this dress for you. That black rag needs washing, or disposing of.'
'*No!* I can't, I *no!*'
'Then breakfast is ready,' Pamela told her, suspiciously.
'I'm not hungry!' She didn't eat for the rest of the day.

That night, there were crashes and bangs downstairs. Pamela drew her gun. The stairs groaned under her weight. Something darted in front of her. Instantly she pulled the trigger and the bullet sped towards the figure, but it didn't stop. The figure wasn't solid. Pamela stepped closer. She gasped. It was the girl! 'But why didn't it . . . ?' the words rushed out of her mouth like a babbling brook.
'Oh please, even a simpleton could work it out. I'm not even alive! I died of grief at my Robert's funeral. To die at another's send off from life means you can never rest. Grief is all I feel. The only way to cease existing is to never have been born . . .'
Pamela was silent for a moment. 'Why were there massive noises down here?' she inquired.
'I was trying to find and destroy my birth certificate. I used to live here.'
'I know where the papers are kept,' Pamela announced.

A short while later, Pamela set down an old portfolio. Inside were a few worn sheets. The girl flipped through them until she found a large card reading *Clarissa Morland.*

Clarissa lay down upon the couch as Pamela tossed the certificate into the fire. At that time, a child was stillborn.

Bryony Thomas (11)
Castlefields Primary School

DEAD OR ALIVE?

Katlin Jones was an average ten-year-old until one day something changed her life.

It was a beautiful summer's evening in July. Katlin and Lucy were bored, it was the summer holidays. They were watching TV when they had a phone call. It was advertising a day out at a power station, so they ordered tickets.

Katlin was on a bus with her friend and they were on their way to the power station. It was a public visit to look round the power station.

On her way round she dropped her wallet through the fence. She was just about to get it when she saw a sign which read *Danger, electricity can kill!* 'Lucy, what can I do! My wallet has fallen through the fence. It's got my bus fare in it.' Katlin quickly slipped through the fence, while Lucy kept guard. Suddenly, Lucy heard the most almighty scream. She whipped round to see Katlin lying on the floor. Her hair was sticking up as if she'd seen a ghost.

One of the guards had heard the scream and came running. He was tall and had blond hair. His father was a well-known baker who owned a shop in town. The guard took out his mobile and called for an ambulance. After a few minutes it arrived.

Poor Katlin, she was in hospital for two weeks. Lucy visited Katlin in hospital. She looked so pale and had the biggest scar anyone could ever have. It was a horrible purple colour. Katlin was a short lady when she'd finished growing. (She had a scar across her chest and would have for evermore).

Rhian Wright (11)
Castlefields Primary School

THE DREAM HUNTER

The year's 1605. Guy Fawkes had committed his audacious crime. He was preparing for his execution on the block.

'Y'know you don't have to do this,' Guy Fawkes remarked. 'If you do I'll haunt your closest relatives in the year 2000, in their dreams.'

'Calm down, the crowd want a good execution t'day,' ordered the executioner.

'Expect no sympathy from me!' he screamed.

The year is 2000.

Steve and Josh were twins whose appearance was similar. They weren't identical but similar enough to play a great joke on someone. (The difference was in Steve's eyes which reflected his character, being bold and daring. Josh was exactly the opposite.) They both liked their lives except for one thing . . . At night, since the start of the year, Steve and Josh had nightmares about an unorthodox being. In their dreams the ghostly man had a burgundy rake. The spikes gritted their teeth and ripped, ripped.

One morning, both woke up with a terrible fright. First action was to dress, but the previous night, Steve and Josh had seen a petrifying sight, so across their chest was a horrendous scar.

'We have to do something!' squealed Josh.

'I've got it,' planned Steve.

That night, Steve knew exactly what to do but was annoyed as they were in an unusual place in their dream. As usual, Guy Fawkes, the ghost, was waiting for the twins.

'Prepare to be hung, drawn and quartered,' growled the twins. Quickly they both dreamt that Guy was hung, then drawn, then quartered.

'I'll be back . . .' he whimpered, then died.

Iain Berryman (10)
Castlefields Primary School

JUST LIFE!

The television buzzed with laughter as the comedy unfolded, but then, with no warning, the programme was cut short by 'News 28'.

The television showed pictures of a burnt building that criminals had set alight. The three girls, who so far had been enjoying a sleepover, fell silent. They were horrified.
'How could someone do such a horrible thing?' Grace whispered over the silence of the night.

The three girls stared at each other. They knew that they could do something to help. It would mean going to the mad scientist, Mr McKay.

The next day the girls strode down the side road heading towards Mr McKay's laboratory. Outside the laboratory was one of his weird inventions, it was bubbling and boiling.
'It wouldn't hurt if we just had a tiny go on it,' laughed Olivia mischievously.
'O-okay then, as long as it's safe,' sighed Maizie.
The door creaked open and they entered. It felt like a rocket.
'Get out! I think it's blowing up,' screamed Grace.
Maizie, Olivia and Grace jumped out to find themselves in a white room full of bubbles.
'G-gh-*ghosts*!' shouted Maizie.
'We are just memories in people's minds, just like everything else in Dreamland,' cackled one of the ghosts as they chased the girls into a bubble of dreams.
'These are the dreams that can be used to improve the world,' cried Grace.

The girls gathered up the dreams and popped the bubble. They ran to the machine.

Later, they proudly explained to the Prime Minister their thoughts and experiences.
'Well done,' he congratulated them. 'Maybe a better world is possible.'

Sophie Attwell (11)
Castlefields Primary School

THE AXEMAN

John stuffed his freezing cold hands in his coat pockets as he shivered in the bitterly cold wind, which was pounding on his face in silent anger. He stopped. The towering trees either side of him, with their amber leaves limp, quivered in a gust of wind. John was sure he'd heard something, a crunch. He carried on hunching his shoulders, keeping his head down. Listening. *Crunch!* Something was there. Slowly he turned his head around and looked down the tree-flanked lane, nothing was there. Snapping his head round John started to run.

Finally reaching the house he found the door unlocked. 'Hello! Anybody there!'
Nothing stirred. John swung the creaking, old door open shedding a little light into the dingy hall. He flicked the light on shutting the door behind him.

He kicked off his shoes and padded into the kitchen where he made a cup of cocoa to calm his nerves. He padded into the living room sinking into the red sofa. He sighed in comfort and then switched on the TV. Then a screeching scrape sent a ripple of cold fear down John's spine. What on earth was that? Then John heard a rattling coming from the hallway. He hadn't locked the door. Someone was coming in. . . .

John jumped up. 'Who's there?' he stuttered, peering into the darkness of the hall. Then, to his absolute horror, a figure draped in darkness started to approach him, axe in hand. John backed up against the wall accidentally switching the light on. It was his dad.
'What are you doing Dad?'
'Ran out of wood. You look like you've seen a ghost!'
'Something like that,' John chuckled.

Olivia Warren (11)
Castlefields Primary School

ICY TROUBLE

Andy and Ryan were on their way home from an enjoyable football training. Eager to reach Andy's house they increased their speed. On their journey, they had to dodge patches of newly formed ice.
'Look!' exclaimed Andy. 'The pond has frozen over!'
'It's massive,' commended Ryan.
'*I dare you* to walk onto the centre of the ice,' ordered Andy.

Ryan trembled, he knew Andy would think he was a wimp if he didn't go on the ice. Therefore, Ryan stepped onto the edge of the ice, shaking like jelly and slowly slid his way to the centre. 'Look, I'm at the centre!' bellowed Ryan. Unfortunately, as Ryan was talking, the ice below him was breaking, any second Ryan would fall into the icy water.

Ryan had vanished. Andy immediately ran onto the ice, not worrying about his life, only about Ryan's. He approached the place where Ryan had fallen and delved his hands into the perishing water, feeling for something solid.

A few seconds later, Andy found Ryan and craned him up by the arms. Quickly, Andy sped off the ice with Ryan in his arms and laid him down on the safe ground.

Suddenly, Andy remembered that his mum had given her mobile to him to ring her if football training wasn't on. Andy rang 999 and asked for an ambulance.

Two minutes later, the ambulance arrived with sirens as loud as stomping elephants. The doctors told Andy that Ryan had to go to the hospital immediately.

When Ryan and Andy were at the hospital the doctors phoned Ryan and Andy's parents and informed them Ryan had pneumonia.

Luckily, Ryan recovered rapidly, and after a month he was allowed to sleep at Andy's house every other Saturday.

Becky Harris (11)
Castlefields Primary School

ARE YOU SCARED OF THE DARK?

I loved the sound of camping a few months ago. But now I only have to look at the scar and I almost faint because I am so scared.

It all happened on a bright summer's day, Peter, Keith and I were hunting for somewhere to set up camp. We found a clearing and pitched our tents. Keith had lit a crackling, roaring fire and we toasted marshmallows. Before we knew it, it was dark.
'Night,' muttered Keith.
'Night,' Peter and I replied in unison.

I wriggled and squirmed about and the lights went out in the boys' tent after a while. I glanced at my watch - 10 o'clock already! I needed the toilet. After a while, I decided I must go, but I was scared, I could hear strange noises, like the trees blowing in the wind - swooping, crunching and whistling. I didn't know if I needed to go now. In the end I grasped my halogen torch and pushed the button. I unzipped my tent and stepped out into the wilderness.
Crunch.
What was that, I thought, *oh, it's only me.*

I ventured into the deep, dark woods and stood behind a tree. But then . . . *Crunch. Crunch.* I heard somebody coming towards me, getting quicker and quicker. *Crunch. Crunch. Crunch.* I began to run. My heart beat like a pounding drum. I ran quicker than a cheetah that night - I'm sure. I turned around and stopped, I saw a glint, a glint of a knife . . .

Katie Ward (11)
Castlefields Primary School

BAD DAY FOR BECKHAM

'Oh David you're awake at last,' cried Victoria, kissing Beckham on the nose.

'It's the day of the big match today isn't it?' groaned Beckham.

'Yes babe, wait here while I go and get your breakfast.'

Beckham sat up and waited for his breakfast. When it came he only ate the toast. He said he wasn't hungry, I personally think it was Victoria's cooking.

An hour later Beckham frantically started to search for his lucky Thomas the Tank Engine socks. 'I can't find them anywhere,' raged Beckham stamping his foot like a baby in a paddy.

'David stop it, you'll ruin the carpet!' Victoria shouted.

'Where are my lucky socks?' questioned Beckham.

'I don't know!' Victoria remarked, calming down.

Soon they'd searched all round their four-storey house. Suddenly Romeo started to cry.

'I must go and see if Romeo and Brooklyn are OK!'

Ten minutes later . . .

'Becks come and look at what I've found, it's your lucky socks.'

'Thanks Vic,' blushed Beckham.

They set off to the stadium. They were playing against Liverpool. It was going to be a tough match!

Two hours later joyful cries could be heard.

'Man U won! Man U won! Man U won!'

Beckham had scored two goals and Scholes had scored one.

'Let's go to bed,' smiled Beckham, 'it's been a hard day.'

Within ten minutes they were both asleep.

Danielle Butterworth (11)
Castlefields Primary School

CAPTURED

'Fetch me my crown, now,' ordered Samuel Slike, master of Moloney Hill.

Mr Slike was a barbaric mole, that treated other moles like dirt. He killed other moles treacherously if they put a foot out of place! Many moles were badly scarred by disgraceful punishment.

Samuel Slike never took off his burgundy stockings and dark grey shorts. His scarlet waistcoat and gold-buttoned shirt was an expensive item of clothing.

Something about today is strange, he thought. His hand was drawing ever nearer to his diamond-handled dagger. Suddenly a snap of a twig stabbed his ears. Something was there!

'Weapons down, Mr S Slike, or else you'll have to face this knife!' threatened a black figure, with a dark, cunning hood.

'H-how D-d-arrreee,' stammered Slike, shaking with anger.

Samuel Slike was dragged roughly into Fonferret forest. The figures tied Slike to a tree and left him there as they trudged off to hunt.

'What do we do with him?' asked one black figure.

'I don't know, keep him?' whispered the other.

A few hours later the mysterious figure returned to Slike. They looked around. Where was Slike?'

'What? Where the? How?' stuttered one of the figures, shaking with rage.

'Get him!' the other screamed.

'Hurry up Mr Slike, let's get out of here before we get killed,' cried Slike's hero, Gundil. Slike was lost for words.

'There is Molery Hill!' Gundil exclaimed. There was Molery Hill!

'It's home, it's home,' Slike shouted joyfully. Slike thought for a moment. What was he like to people? He just noticed. It happened to him. He was now one of the kindest moles that lived. Molery Hill lived in peace.

Emma Askins (10)
Castlefields Primary School

A Day In The Life Of The Creature In The Garden Pond

The creature in the garden pond snarled in ravenous hunger. Spit dripping from his malicious canines. Stalking his defenceless prey, preparing to lunge. And . . .

'Wake up junior,' the creature boomed, surprising his unsuspecting son.

'Aw, Dad. Do you have to pounce on me every morning? It's not even breakfast time.'

'Well if you just wait here, then I'll bring you some delicious, juicy goldfish. I'm sure you'd like that.'

The creature in the garden pond lived with his small family amongst the reeds and water grasses at the bottom of the human's lawn. The creature in the garden pond only killed what he needed. He took a few plump goldfish back to his wife and his son. When they had eaten their fill, the creature in the garden pond told them of humans and their strange contraptions, their televisions and their microwaves, their telephones and their gadgets.

Before long, it was lunchtime. The creature in the garden pond knew what to do, as usual, he covered himself in water lilies and bulrushes. At noon, the human came, right on cue. He was carrying a bucket of fish feed as he strolled down the garden. Closer, closer, suddenly, a vision of terror leapt from the pond and unleashed a deafening roar. Petrified, the human fled in horror. Leaving the vast bucket of fish feed to be consumed within the jaws of the creature in the garden pond, and his family.

I wonder if the humans will ever find out about the dark secrets which the garden pond conceals, or the terrifying family which live there?

Phil West (11)
Castlefields Primary School

Catch Him If You Can!

Saturday, 18th June hadn't began too well. David had teased his sister, causing an argument. Amelia spilt her milk on Benny, their dog. So the day didn't look good. Amelia was an 8-year-old. She was particularly moody today. Her 10-year-old brother, David, was also moody and stubborn.

'Mum! I'm taking Benny for a walk,' David shouted.

'Well take Amelia with you.'

'Oh! If I have to?'

Amelia and David strolled out of the door.

A while later, they arrived at the town hall.

'Can I hold Benny?' Amelia asked.

'Yes, but be careful,' David answered. He handed Amelia the lead. Suddenly, Benny wriggled free and bounded off. 'No! Benny! Come back!' David yelled.

David and Amelia had begun to search for Benny in the park. It was particularly busy that day, as it was a weekend.

'Oh, great!' David moaned sarcastically. David could see plenty of other dogs enjoying their walk. He'd never find Benny in such a crowd.

'This is all your fault,' he groaned at Amelia.

'I couldn't help it,' she whimpered.

'Never mind . . . Look! There's Benny!' David cried.

Benny was digging savagely in the bushes. David and Amelia sped over to him.

Without warning, a woman stepped out from behind a tree and they collided into her.

'Sorry,' they mumbled.

'Well you should watch where you're going,' the woman said indignantly.

David and Amelia ran off before she could say anything else. Benny had disappeared again. But as they rounded the corner, they saw him.

'Gotcha!' David muttered. 'Come on. Let's get home before Mum gets back!'

Catherine Tennant (11)
Castlefields Primary School

A Day In The Life Of Count Dracula

Scanning the town high and low, around estates and between dustbins, all for dinner. Lovely, ruby, juicy blood is a great way to calm your stomach. Well at least I think it is . . . ooooh there's my first victim. Down I go . . .
'Arghhh! My neck!'
Ha ha! The mayor of darkness triumphs again! Transylvanian blood is very rich you know! Better than Uncle Batt's victims at least. When I went to visit him in Cleveland I threw up over a cargo ship in the Atlantic. It took a whole week to get the taste of sour bubbling blood out of my fangs.

I don't get humans. I honestly don't. They call us bloodthirsty creatures that prey on them! Well you would too if you hadn't a bite to eat *all day!* And they prey on foxes and eat lamb and beef too. Anyway . . . there's a lovely lady about to be sentenced as my dessert.
'Aaaargh! Not me! I'm so young -'

Well that's sorted. I'm off back to my crib now. Away from the world in my warm, cosy coffin. Err, sorry I had an episode again.

Here we are, do you like it? No seriously? My coffin's over there by my gold-studded mantelpiece! And below is my *secret sanctuary* for private business. Oh. It's dawn, I'd better be sleeping now, see you.

Joe Travis (11)
Crowmoor Primary School

A Day In The Life Of God

As I woke up I thought that I would make a planet. I can tell you I searched everywhere, high and low, in corners and in holes. Then I saw a black ball and I thought that would be the planet for me. I said, 'Let there be light,' and there was.

Once I had given light to Earth I separated the seas from the sky and I called the sky, Heaven.

The third day I made all the flowers and trees and grass. You should have seen the flowers. They were all different colours of the rainbow.

The fourth day I made night for people to rest. I also made stars including the sun.

Day five I made colourful fish to swim in the seas, lakes and streams and the birds to fly in the sky.

The sixth day I said, 'Let there be animals, like elephants and cows to give us milk and butter.' Also I made Adam and Eve and left them in charge.

And on the seventh day I left the world to rest and me too of course.

Lisa Tudor (11)
Crowmoor Primary School

WHO'S TALKING?

'Now what do I do? I'm so bored. Nan said they had lovely paintings here. But all I can see is miserable, dull paintings.' Then Eddie went and had a good moan.
'Oh Eddie stop moaning,' Eddie's nan said, in a great big puff.

As Eddie dawdled upstairs he saw a brilliant painting in a small room at the top of the stairs. It was blue, green and red and so on. There were so many colours. Unfortunately though he didn't see any more that he liked. When it was time for Eddie to move on he went round this really bendy corner (that had horrible wallpaper) and then he saw this big room so he ran over. Eddie had a good look around the room but there was nothing that came to his interest. As Eddie had a good look around he saw this horrible picture in the corner, 'Err that is ugly!' he said.

As he was walking round all day his legs were aching so he sat down on a bench. Just as he sat down he heard a voice from the room. But no one else was in there. So he whispered, 'Hello who's talking?'
'It's me in the corner, I'm in the picture.'
'A talking picture.'

Eddie ran to get his nan. When he found her he pulled her to the room and started to speak to it. But it didn't say anything. Eddie's nan was mad. 'You pulled me all this way for nothing!' she shouted.

Kelly Davies (11)
Crowmoor Primary School

A DAY IN THE LIFE OF MILES 'TAILS' PROWLER

What I'm going to do is tell you about my tenth birthday since that is quite amusing!

It all started as a surprise birthday party but that is gonna take too long so I'm going to skip to the part where I blew out the candles. I vanquished out the flames one by one until I got to the last. When I blew it out the flame fell onto Amy's dress and, at that moment, she started to shriek and shout. Knuckles started to beat the fire out but the flames on Amy's dress didn't die away, instead the flames spread onto Knuckles' tail! Now there were two people running around like idiots!

Then I searched for Sonic but he was nowhere to be found. But then again I did find him, he was choking . . . from laughter!

So it's not amusing? Then what about this! Amy and Knuckles were running around so much that they began to feel woozy. They soon tripped over Sonic, who was going to die in a matter of moments. I decided to stop this and then I got a bucket of water to do so!

Then I hurled it at Amy and Knuckles! Though it also wet Sonic in the process! It got worse after that. Sonic and Amy started to chase me! Knuckles doesn't care about being wet so he didn't join the chase. (Thank goodness!)

So it all ended in a huge killer chase! (I was the prey) Anyway believe me that wasn't the worse day I ever had!

Syeda Faiza Islam (11)
Crowmoor Primary School

A Day In The Life Of Granny (Who Got Eaten By The Big Bad Wolf)

'Oh good Red Riding Pud is coming. I'd better put my teeth in. Now I can speak, that's better.'

Today is Sunday and Little Red Riding Hood is coming to see her granny. Little Red Riding Hood is on her way when she meets *Bernard Wolf.*

'Hello little girl and where are you going?' Little Red Riding Hood tells Bernard she is going to Granny's, and Bernard knows where Granny lives so he runs to her house and asks her to go out, and to give him some clothes, so she does.

Soon Little Red Riding Hood walks in when, suddenly, Bernard eats her. Then Granny walks in and knows just what has happened.
'Oh never mind! She was a nuisance anyway, coming here every day!'
So it was still a happy ending!

Joanne Egglestone (10)
Crowmoor Primary School

A DAY IN THE LIFE OF MISS MUFFET

Spiders are horrid creatures! I don't think I'll be able to sit on that tuffet again because how will I know that it's gone? It's probably sitting behind it right now, waiting for me and when I do come out he'll pounce on me. Anyway I'll tell you what exactly happened because you've probably heard all the different versions. Now here goes . . .

I was sitting in my kitchen waiting for my curds and whey. When it was ready I went to the bottom of the garden and sat on my tuffet. All I had to do was eat a small spoonful and then . . . and then it happened, out of nowhere came the most scariest, the most dariest, the most hairiest spider, dangling on its web. As soon as I saw it I threw my curds and whey up in the air and messed up my favourite pink frilly dress. How disappointed I was!

After that incident I have had a spider detector and haven't seen a spider for ages, but then my scream probably scared them off.

At bedtime, before I get into bed, I scan round my bedroom walls and floor just in case a spider is creeping around.

All in all, I think that spiders are a waste of time and should be taken out of this world and moved onto a planet of their own.

Rebecca Mogg (11)
Crowmoor Primary School

AT THE SHORE

Staring down at the golden sand, Joe felt the hot summer sun blazing down on him. Straight ahead he could see the glittering sand dunes.

Grabbing hold of the spade Joe began to dig a hole. Even though the sun was blistering there was still a cool breeze. All around all Joe could hear was children shouting with excitement. By now Joe was tired of digging so he decided to go up the sand dunes.

Running as fast as his short, plump legs could carry him, Joe ran towards the sand dune. On his way Joe glanced at a small child that had fallen over he thought about helping her but carried on running. 'Poor child,' Joe muttered under his breath.

As soon as Joe got to the sand dunes something strange happened . . . the sun waned and the sky grew grey and the beach suddenly looked deserted.

Looking around he saw a big black figure staring down at the sea. Its hood was pointed and its face was black. Joe gulped. The tall, dark figure began to walk slowly towards him. Gently walking backwards Joe's heart began to race.

'Hello Joe,' whispered the tall, dark figure.
'H-h-hello,' Joe said shocked.
Getting closer by the minute the figure began to cackle. Effortlessly the figure pulled down its hood . . . it was Joe's auntie. They both started to laugh and then they walked home.

Siân Scott-Ridgway (11)
Crowmoor Primary School

THE BLACK FIGURE

'Do we have to go?' cried Lucy packing her bags into the boot of the car.

'Yes. Now I don't want to hear anything about it,' shouted her mum angrily.

Blushing, Lucy clambered into her dad's *seven* seater. Why, oh why he needed a seven seater when there was only four of them, it was such a big car.

As it was such a hot day Lucy, her little sister Sam, Mum and Dad had finished packing. They were sunbathing. Her two kittens were playing in the shade. Finally it was time to leave and Lucy was whining.

At last down in Kent Road . . .

'It's a big, big house,' cried Lucy running down the pathway towards the house.

Soon it was very late and it was Lucy's bedtime. In bed Lucy took off her glasses and went to sleep.

At midnight Lucy woke to a sudden creak. It was the floorboard. Tiptoeing to the door she peered out. *A big black figure* was coming closer and closer every minute.

Lucy wondered whether her baby sister Sam was OK. Shutting the bedroom door, the handle started to shake the monster was about to come. The door creaked wide open, she hid under the bedcover. The thing was lifting up the cover, the finger, the nail varnish . . . *nail varnish? . . .*

'Phew it's only Mum!'

Chelsea Carvell (11)
Crowmoor Primary School

IF PICTURES COULD SPEAK . .

I love art, but it sounds so boring walking through an old building with pictures in it. It was my mother who dragged me to this exhibition.

Pulling myself through the first room, out loud I sarcastically murmured, 'Wow! How exciting! Three girls on a merry-go-round! I could see that at the fair!'
Mum was going to hit me, but instead warningly whispered, 'Shut up!' Then walked out the pale, dusty room, I was by myself.

Turning round, I stared out of the window.
'All day and night I'm in this pose and someone laughs at me! It isn't fair!' squeaked a voice.
My heart pounded. I was all alone, so where was the voice coming from? Staring at the merry-go-round picture I realised the girls were talking! Then they beckoned at me. Slowly I walked forward. I was in the picture! *Brilliant!* I thought. Fairground rides everywhere! Being a ten-year-old this was great! But what was I going to do? Mum would be finished looking round by now. Luckily one of the girls told me I could stop time. I supposedly stopped time and went on everything! But soon I had to go.

Hopping out of the picture, Mum walked in.
'Quick! Let's get in the car!' called Mum, pulling me towards the front door. Driving home, Mum moaned that she hated it! So I asked, 'Could we go again?'
We burst out laughing.

Dulcie-May Parcell (11)
Crowmoor Primary School

AT THE WATER'S EDGE . . .

The sun was sizzling and people at the beach were building sandcastles, swimming and sunbathing. But there was one thing strange. There was a man standing by the rocks. He had a long, black cloak, which covered his face. It was the length of his whole body. His hands were bony and his fingers were thin. The wind ruffled his cloak

Nearby there was a boy building a sandcastle. He stopped. He saw the man, his body shuddered. There were hardly any people on the beach. Suddenly the boy heard something in the wind. It sounded like it was whispering his name; 'Michael,' it whispered.
Quickly Michael picked up his bucket and spade, walked to his mom and said, 'M-Mommy c-c-can I go h-home n-n-now?;
'Of course you can,' his mom replied.

The next day Michael went back to the beach and so did the strange man, still wearing the same clothes. The same thing happened the next day, and the next, and weeks after. The strange figure was still there.

One morning Michael was in his room, getting ready to go to the beach (like he had done every day). But today was different. Today Michael was going to say hello to the strange figure.
'Hurry up Michael!' shouted his mom from downstairs.
'Finished!' Michael shouted back.

It wasn't long before they got to the beach. Michael ran straight over to the rocks. He stopped, the man wasn't there. All that there was, was his cloak and a pile of dust . . .

Bobbie-Jane Carter (11)
Crowmoor Primary School

A Day In The Life Of Jamie (Who Killed The Jabberwocky)

In a mysterious land, on the edge of a cliff, lived a young boy called Jamie. He lived with his father called George. His father told him to be careful because people had seen a big green thing. People said it was a Jabberwocky, others said it was a giant. The description of it was it had red flaming eyes, teeth as big as bricks and claws as sharp as knives.

Jamie wanted to go for a walk in the wood so he did. He was walking and everything was quiet then he approached an apple tree with juicy apples on, they were also ripe. Jamie picked off an apple and ate it. He thought it was tasty and juicy.

A big sound of thunder came, well not exactly thunder, it was a really big footstep and Jamie wobbled. *Then* coming through the trees was a green thing. It had teeth as big as bricks, claws as sharp as knives and red-hot flaming eyes. So Jamie casually took out his vorpal sword and chopped the Jabberwocky's head off and put it in the bag.

He went home and told his dad and his dad was very happy with him and he said, 'Well done you defeated the Jabberwocky. I'm proud of you,' he added.
So that was it! Everyone was happy.

Jade McMullen-Jones (11)
Crowmoor Primary School

A DAY IN THE LIFE OF MARY JONES

One fine morning Mary Jones made the decision to go and buy a Bible
. . .

By lunchtime every step that Mary had taken blistered and bruised her
bare feet. Mary looked around her. The hostile environment had seemed
to cloud her. As Mary walked along the road she tried to remember the
times when she had read the Bible with Mr and Mrs Evans. She could
remember those days so clearly. *Nearly there,* she told herself and she
walked on.

A few hours later Mary came to a small stream and thought that it
would be a good idea to cool down her feet. Then after a long, well-
earned rest, she started walking again.

Mary had grown more and more weak and weary but . . . finally . . .
after twenty-five miles of walking . . . she had arrived in Bala.

Mary soon came to Mr Charles' shop. Before Mary went in she put on
her best shoes and took a deep breath. With no hesitation Mary had
taken a step into the shop.
She smiled, 'Excuse me but do you have any Bibles?' she blushed.
'I'm sorry I just sold the last one and any others you see have been
promised to other people,' Mr Charles smiled.
Disappointment swept over Mary. She turned and walked away.
'Wait!' said Mr Charles and he disappeared into the back room. When
he returned he was holding a little black book . . . a Bible!

Mary turned her back on Bala and happily made her way home holding
her Bible as tight as possible.

Samantha Louise Preston (11)
Crowmoor Primary School

DON'T GO DOWN THE WOODS

One rainy day there was Emma, Richard, Danni and Jack sitting in the house at Horsehay, 3b Connormara Meadows. The rain stopped so they went outside and walked along a slippery path. Suddenly they got lost up in a forest. They could not find their way out.

It turned dark, night settled in the sky.
Jack said, 'What's that noise over there?'
Emma said, 'What noise?' Suddenly she noticed she was in a ghost zone with her friends and there was no way out.

Danni went down into the forest with Richard to get some wood to make a fire, while Emma and Jack kept guard.
Suddenly Jack felt something in his pocket. He slowly lifted the object out of his pocket and there was a small touch of light shining through the glass of the torch.

When Richard and Danni got back the noise began to vibrate on the floor. All of them sat together on a log. A white shape appeared in front of them. They were all frightened of it. Jack said, 'Let's put the wood on the ground and make the fire.'
Emma lit the match to make a fire.

ghosts appeared all around them, suddenly a man came with a machine and he sucked them into a jar. He said, 'Come on kids. I will take you home, you need some sleep . . .'

Emma Henfield (11)
Dawley CE Primary School

THE DAY I MET MY BEST FRIEND

Tuesday 18th October 1994

It started when we were both three and I had just started nursery. I had met a new friend, her name is Samantha. She had got light brown hair with bluey-green eyes and little ears. I had seen her before though, because her nan lived opposite my house.

When we sat down for our biscuits and drink, I looked at her and I could see that she was nervous too. Samantha said hello to me and I said it back to her and from then on we have been best buddies. All we ever do is play in the sandpits or open cupboards and wait for the surprise to hit our heads.

She was like a sister to me and I was like a brother to her. Samantha came to every party I had and she's my best friend and hopefully will be when I am older.

Monday 2nd June 2003

Me and Sam aren't as close as we used to be. I have my other friends and she has hers. Sometimes we chat and have fun. On some occasions we were not friends but really we will always be friends.

Sam and I are in Year 6 and are leaving in six weeks, we are going to the same secondary school and I hope our friendship will last. And I will keep the best memories of her forever.

Christopher Hull (11)
Dawley CE Primary School

THROUGH THE PORTAL

Jamie was playing football on his own. He didn't have any friends at school. Everyone made fun of his gingery hair. But this was all to change. Jamie kicked the ball in his anger. The ball soared high in the air and landed in the . . . woods! Jamie sighed and went in search of his ball.

When Jamie got to the edge of the woods he felt scared. He looked around for a stick to defend himself with in case there were any bad things in there. So he went into the woods. All light faded, except for some openings here and there. Suddenly Jamie noticed something in the corner of his eye. It was a . . . a . . . *portal!* Jamie was amazed. He ran over to it and stared at it for several minutes. At last he walked into it not knowing what he was doing.

When Jamie got out of the portal he gasped for air. He was on top of the clouds! And there, in the distance, was his ball. But before he could do anything a dozen ninjas popped up from the clouds. Without thinking he swiped with his stick and the ninjas were gone. *That was easy,* he thought. And so he made his way to his ball, battling the ninjas. Jamie grabbed his ball and went back through the portal.

The next day he went to school and told everyone about his journey. Now he was the most popular boy in the school!

Daniel Bell (10)
Dawley CE Primary School

THE TRIP THAT WENT WRONG

James woke up later than usual because he had missed his alarm clock. As soon as he got up he got dressed, and he, and his family went to the theme park.

When he got there he was so excited, he rushed ahead to see the new ride. It was called 'Pirate Neville's Voyage'. It sounded really cool because James really liked pirates. His dad, mum and his sister went off.

James couldn't wait to go on the ride, but he noticed something strange. People were getting on the ride, but they weren't coming off. James picked up a stick and shoved it in his pocket. James queued up for the new ride. As he got in the boat, he opened both eyes as wide as he could.

When the ride started, he cold hear a laughing sound coming from inside of the tunnel. All of a sudden a pirate jumped out and captured everyone and hid them in the tunnel. James only had a little stick with him. People were screaming and shouting but it was no use. He threw the stick and it hit a window. The sun shone through the window and all the pirates disappeared.

They all went back into the ship and went to the end of the ride. When Mum and Dad found out they didn't believe him until it was in the newspaper and on TV.
James and his family never went there again.

Would you go on that ride?

Chris Lumbard (11)
Dawley CE Primary School

A NEW WORLD

One cold autumn day there was a little ghost sitting by a brown crumbly tree. It had a black hole so the little ghost could just get in. The little ghost was so cold he couldn't even move, the little ghost started to think of where he wanted to be.

Then the little ghost said in a quiet voice, 'I wish I was in a safe place.' Then it happened. The ghost had vanished into thin air, like a rocket into space. Then the little ghost found himself somewhere else, it was not even raining hard.

The little ghost was looking round to see if there was anybody around. Then a young girl was running towards the little ghost and then they bumped into each other. The young girl brushed the dust off and looked at the ghost, the ghost looked at the girl. The ghost asked her name. The girl said, 'My name is Jessica,' and the ghost and Jessica became great friends, but something really strange happened - a big flash and the ghost had gone.

It was a mystery which was never solved but Jessica would always think of the ghost. The little ghost was safe - he was with his family and he would never forget his best friend Jessica.

Jade Fiddler (11)
Dawley CE Primary School

THE FORGOTTEN HOUSE

Down the street and around the corner is an old, forgotten bridge. Walking under it, across a snarling lake, past the thorns and overgrown weeds is a broken footpath. If you walk down the footpath you will see an old, slimy pond with weed as tall as yourself. If you walk up a bit more you will see lots of trees. It's like they are reaching out to grab you and there in the distance is an old, smelly house.

The walls outside the house are mouldy and the windows are all smashed in. The tiles are sliding off the roof and the door is tied shut with blood-red roses climbing up. If you pull off the roses and push the door open, it will slam against the walls, of which you can see the water running down. If you step on the floor it makes a slushing noise. If you walk into the living room you'll see it's partly falling down. If you look up you will see a hole up in the bathroom and if you pull up the carpet and open the hatch you will see the ghosts.

I bet you're wondering how I know. Well, you'll see . . .

Simon Saunders (11)
Dawley CE Primary School

THE MYSTERIOUS NOISES

Stomp! Stomp! Stomp! That's all Jo and Sam heard all night. Jo turned
on his watch light. He told Sam miserably the time.
'3.16am now Sam.'
By then Sam had fallen asleep. Suddenly there was a bang at the door.
'Argh! Help me Sam!' Jo had gone.

The next morning Sam had a fright at the sight of Jo's blood. It was
terrifying. On the news the headline was, 'Murder is a hobby in Noble
town!' The headline was in every newspaper in town because of the
mysterious murder of a nine-year-old boy. The question was, who was
the next victim going to be?

Another murder! It was Sam's best friend Jamie. He was found in the
scrapyard. Only blood and bones were found. There was someone going
around killing people and the local police were nowhere to be found.
People were going out of business and the town was going broke.

Everyone was going out of sight. A group of friends saw a fiendish
beast. A trap was set for the beast. A net was put on a balcony. The
children were rescued by the trap that they had set. But no one knows
where the beast has been taken.

Gavin Brooks (11)
Dawley CE Primary School

A BLAZE OF MAGIC

Danielle was an ordinary girl, aged 11, not much to tell about her really apart from she's my best friend. She's simply the best person in the world to be mates with.

By the way, I'm Emma Henfield and I'm about to tell you about our shopping spree. Now boys - you must have thought, *uh oh!* when you heard the word *shopping*. But trust me, fashion does not occur here.

Me and Danielle were waiting about town, when she walked up to the doll store. Now when I saw the glimmer in Dan's eyes, I knew she was excited, but over what? Zonks! A rag doll.

The doll had pretty pink cheeks and red lips, blue eye make-up on with long, luscious lashes. She had a pretty pink dress on which had white flowers all over it. Also white and pink lace-up shoes to match. Her hair was silky brown with long slick curls to finish at the end.

Now when Danielle gets excited she goes hyper. She frustratedly pulled out a wad of money from her pocket and threw it at the shopkeeper, literally. Then grabbing the doll she rushed out of the shop, leaving me behind.

From then on the Groves, Danielle's family, came from the richest and most popular people in town to the poorest and strangest family. Soon after this the Groves moved away and you wouldn't believe it but I never saw or heard from Danielle again.

Dan would not have just left me - was that coincidental or maybe . . . magic!

Poppy Durnall (10)
Dawley CE Primary School

A DAY IN THE LIFE OF A CAT

Well cats are quite strange I think. But I've always wanted to be one, only for a day though. So now I have my chance to be one and everyone will call me Missie.

'Miaow, miaow!' I cried. I was hungry and I didn't know how to say it, so I ran to my dish and miaowed.

After a while, a little girl came in and fed me. She had blonde hair and blue eyes, I thought that she would fuss me at night. So I was trying to get the hang of this licking the bowl business. I stood by the door and cried.

The little girl let me outside. I went into the muddy part of outside and dug a hole in which to do my business.

I walked off and found another cat, it was a ginger one. It pounced on me and scratched me, so I had a fight with it. There were a few hairs on the ground, but we were both alright.

I decided that I was going to go inside and have some fuss from that little girl. I walked to the door and miaowed again and I scratched the window of the door.

The little girl let me in and gave me a stroke, well maybe for about a half an hour, then it was time for me to turn back into me again - so I did!

Erika Peake (10)
Dawley CE Primary School

A DAY IN THE LIFE OF MY SISTER

I was kneeling on the cold, wooden floor and I was very annoyed. My younger sister Lauren, stared at me, wide-eyed.

'What's the matter Kirst? You've got nothing to be annoyed about. All you have to do is a few chores, then you go out,' quizzed Lauren.
'Easy!' I screamed. 'But I do way more than a few chores, you don't!'
'At least you don't get treated like a baby. I know, let's switch places for the week, shall we?'

So we did and at first it went well . . .

I did all Lauren's homework - it was difficult but I didn't let Lauren know that. I didn't have any homework to give to Lauren as I'm going up to the secondary school after the holidays. That annoyed me.

Lauren did her chores, then went out. I wasn't allowed to, of course! Lauren was enjoying *my* freedom but I hated being cooped up.

Later on, on the third night of our switch, Lauren and I had a massive argument. 'I want to swap back,' I demanded.
'No Kirsty, we agreed and besides it's fun being you!' said Lauren.
'Yes, we are swapping back!' I shouted.
'No!' she said.
'Yes!'
'Fine, but don't expect me to talk you ever again.'
Lauren finally gave in.
'Fine!'

But of course we did talk again . . .
'It's better being you . . . for a while!'

Kirstie Pritchard (11)
Dawley CE Primary School

GHOST STORY

Three friends called Danni, Sophie and Emma went to a funfair in Wales for their holiday.

Finally they arrived and had just come off the ghost train ride when they saw a long string dangling down with something on the end of it.
'It's a game, you know the one, when you pick a string and it's got a coin on the end!' exclaimed Emma.

She ran over to it and found a two pound coin. Sophie grabbed it but as soon as she took her hand away, all the lights went out and it started to rain. The only people around were the three friends.

Danni suggested they went on a ride to take their minds off it and maybe make things right. But as they sat down in the waltzer's cart, they found themselves in the woods.
'What's happening to us?' they all shouted.

They were walking along exploring, when all of a sudden Emma fell over and banged into a tree. As soon as she hit the tree the darkness flashed and it was sunny again and they were back in the funfair.

They never found out what had happened, or why, but one thing's for sure, they will never return there again!

Danielle Groves (11)
Dawley CE Primary School

THE MAN AND HIS TIGER

Down in the darkest wood there is a broken down house with big holes in the roof where there lived a ghost and his tiger. The ghost was half-man and half-horse. This tiger's name was Ripper because he can rip a man to bits in just five seconds.

The man was called Mr Dead, he had a knife which could go straight through your body and he would eat you too.

He hated people on his land. He'd send Ripper after them. Ripper would drag them back and then the man used the knife to kill them. The tiger would then get a treat and eat some of the body.

Mr Dead would get the brains and put them in a jar with all the eyes, ears and mouths. He also steals people's cars. He takes them and drives them down a ditch so that they blow up, so that he leaves no trace . . .

James Fiddler (11)
Dawley CE Primary School

A DAY IN THE LIFE OF MY BEST FRIEND

Dear Diary,

Today Diary, the weirdest thing happened. Jade and I swapped lives. It all happened when we were at school. We were arguing over what to play and then we sort of swapped lives - it was crazy.

Dear Diary,

It was ultra weird. I can't believe we swapped lives. I ran home to tell my mom. But then I thought what if she doesn't believe me?

Dear Diary,

Anyway Diary, I went to sleep but then in the night I woke up and I was me again! That second, my mobile rang, I pushed past my Gareth CDs and picked up my phone. I moved my blonde hair out of the way and answered my phone. It was Jade calling to say she'd changed back. We apologised and said goodnight, then went back to sleep.

Dear Diary,

So Jade and I are best friends again. For now!
At play, we just talk about our little secret. I wonder if anyone would believe us?

Jessica Lovett (11)
Dawley CE Primary School

BERTON MANSION

A long time ago there was an important family who lived in a castle. That's where I'm going to start my story . . .

In the last century, a castle was knocked down and it was said that a ghost lived there. A few months later, the big stone blocks from it were used to build a new castle and once it was built, the Berton family moved into it.

They had two children, one three years old and the other thirteen years old but it wouldn't be long before they left this physical life.

The girl called Ann liked dancing and she found the perfect place to do it, on the roof of the castle. She would go up there every day to dance. and the boy, Thomas, found it fun to run through the halls and up and down the stairs.

One day, the girl walked up to the roof to dance, it had been raining so when she started dancing, she slipped. She had fallen off the side. She was clearly dead, no one could survive a fall like that. Everybody rushed out of the castle on hearing the scream.

Thomas didn't go out because he knew she was dead. Then he saw a ghost coughing, he jumped backwards and began to choke. No one came to help because they were all outside. After a while, he also died and if you visit the castle today you might see the girl dancing on the roof, or the boy running through the halls. If you're lucky, you might see the ghost that coughs a lot too.

Christopher Parry (11)
Dawley CE Primary School

THE GHOST OF CAIRO MANOR

Alex and Ben were pulling up into the drive of their new house. They got out. The house was really old. They walked up the path to the mahogany front door. Their Dad put the key into the lock and turned it. The door creaked open - it was wonderful. It was like a manor house. Wait a minute, it *was* a manor house because Alex and Ben's family had won the lotto, so they decided to buy this house. They unpacked all their stuff in the grand house and settled in.

A few weeks later weird stuff began to happen, a settee moved, music started playing on its own. Alex and Ben expected the worst, they thought the house was haunted. They were right because the next day they saw the ghost - well the teacup he was carrying. They telephoned the Ghost Eliminators and they came the next day.

First they tried sucking him up, then they tried special glue, nothing worked. So they left.

Alex and Ben had a try, first they got him with paint so they were able to see him. Then they got a safe, which everyone knows ghosts can't escape from. They put an automatic closing door on it, which was an elastic band and they put a frisbee in it. The ghost went in and he was caught! They threatened to throw him in the sea, so he slowly walked out of the house, sobbing. They never saw the ghost again.

Martin Pearce (11)
Dawley CE Primary School

A DAY IN THE LIFE OF A DOLPHIN

I woke up and looked about. Why was I in water, loads of water? All these things were rushing through my head, then I looked down, expecting to see a body with legs and feet on the end. But no I just saw water, water, water! Hang on, how was I going to breathe? Oh yes, I had gills and by now I realised that I was a dolphin. I was pleased because they're my favourite animal.

I was swimming about and I met some friends. We were happily swimming when a great white shark came and tried to eat us up. We were swimming like mad but then it caught my friends and I was the only one left.

Suddenly I could not breathe, I was drowning. But no, I was swimming to shore and when I got to shore everyone was asking me questions but all I wanted to do was to go to bed and sleep. But no, more, more, more questions.

Suddenly my mum came and more questions were fired at me about this and about that. Next, news reporters came and they also asked me questions. I just knew what I had to do, run home, get into bed and go to sleep. I knew I would be better in the morning and that is what I did.

Rosie Evans (10)
Fairfield Prep School

A DAY IN THE LIFE OF A HAT SELLER

On a hot sunny day, in an unknown village in Chad, a young hat-seller was selling hats. He had been doing this all morning. At about eleven o'clock he was getting tired so he decided to rest for a moment. Before he could stop himself, he fell asleep.

A few minutes later, a small monkey crept out of the bush and saw the hats lying in the basket next to the hat-seller. He liked the look of the hats and decided to take one! He ran to the nearest tree and ran up it to tell his friends. They immediately wanted one so the monkey led all the rest of the monkeys to get a hat. They each picked up a hat and went up the tree. In all this commotion the hat-seller woke up and saw the monkeys with his hats. He started jumping up and down, getting very annoyed. So did the monkeys. He then started kicking the ground and the monkeys copied him. He started getting really annoyed.

Then he realised that the monkeys were copycats so he threw his hat into the basket and at that, all the other monkeys threw their hats into the basket. When all the hats were in the basket, he picked up the basket and ran as fast as his two legs could carry him, also feeling very relieved!

Rahul Ghelani (10)
Fairfield Prep School

A DAY IN THE LIFE OF A RABBIT

I woke up with a fright. Where was I? It wasn't my own bedroom, that was for sure! I was in a cage with white bars around me. I had long dangling ears and soft, sleek fur, all over my body. It then occurred to me that I was not myself at all, I was a rabbit! I wandered around the small cage and just before I could even get to the bottom right hand corner, I heard a noise.

'Oh my gosh, Mum, quick! There's a rabbit in my room!' she screamed and picked up the cage.

Before I could even move, I found myself being carried towards what looked like a big heap of different colours.
'There you go, you great smelly ball of fluff.'
She threw me down onto the pile of colours but it was not a soft landing and it was not a pile of colours, it was a rubbish dump and it smelt like it too. *Thud!*

I was sitting in the cage after that for about five minutes. Then I felt my long dangling ears disappear and then my soft, sleek coat go and before I knew it, I was myself again. I pushed open the door and ran.

Charlotte Boland (10)
Fairfield Prep School

A DAY IN THE LIFE OF A DRIP

I woke up, I wasn't in my bed. I was in some sort of pipe and I was lying there with others of my shape and size. It was totally quiet, everyone around seemed very used to it. The shining walls were quite dazzling.

Suddenly, someone pressed or turned something and we all came tumbling out, we had to fit through some small holes. I nearly got stuck! So we all came falling out from quite a height for a normal-sized human, but for a drip! I shouted, but nobody heard me. I screamed but still nobody heard so I carried on screaming my head off as we fell, hoping someone would hear.

We suddenly hit a wall, a see-through wall, I looked about me, my sudden panic had faded. I looked up and saw more of my kind fall the way I had, only not screaming their heads off. Then I looked down a bit to see if I was still very high up, my panic almost completely gone now, when suddenly, to my horror, I saw my sister dancing naked. It was then and only then that I realised where I was. I was in the shower and my sister was having her morning shower. I suddenly started laughing out loud, I couldn't stop.

Suddenly everything went blank and I found myself sitting on my bed still laughing and wondering why!

Beatrice Cooper (10)
Fairfield Prep School

A Day In The Life Of A Dog

I woke up to the footsteps of my master. The door handle slowly went down and the kitchen door slowly opened and in came my master. I jumped up at him and he cuddled me. I started to bark because I knew that we were going for a walk.

Before I knew it, the walk was over and I was back at home. Everybody had a busy day so I was on my own. I had something to eat and drink and then I got into my basket and slept for a couple of hours. Just as I was getting into a good dream I was awakened by the front door opening and a voice calling, 'Meg?'

I ran to the front door and jumped up at my master. I guessed it was time for a walk so I ran and got my ball. I was having fun but my master had to go back to work. So I lay by the front door, waiting for someone to come home when I saw a light from a car. The front door opened and in came my master with his wife and children. I loved them all so I played with them.

All of a sudden I was put in my basket because it was night-time. As I was going to sleep I thought that I have a wonderful life.

Hannah Paisley (10)
Fairfield Prep School

A Day In The Life Of A Bottle Of Champagne

Here I am, sitting on the shelf, when a man grabs me by the neck and smothers me in tissue paper. It's really dark. Now there's a screechy noise and a bumpy ride.

I'm taken out of the paper and put into a pretty bag. I have another bumpy ride and then I'm carried into an extremely noisy place. It's full of people, chatting. I'm then placed on the table.

My cork is pulled out and I'm poured into glasses. Everyone takes a glass. There I am, bubbling away when a large man steps out and says, 'Ladies and gentlemen, please be upstanding. The toast is the health and happiness of Annabel Butler.'
'Annabel Butler!'

Well who is this Annabel Butler anyway? She must be special, having all that said about her. I've never had anything like that said about me. I hear a cry. I look to my right. I see a baby. Then I see a lady walk over to the baby.
'What's upsetting little baby Annabel?' she says.

Okay, Annabel is a baby! Why are they throwing a party for a baby? She doesn't exactly do much apart from sit there with people all over her. I suppose there is a point, because a baby is a new life!

I'm pleased to be here because it makes me feel important. My life is at an end because people are drinking me quickly, but Annabel's life is just beginning.

Nathalie Matthews (10)
Fairfield Prep School

A DAY IN THE LIFE OF A POODLE

I wake up at about 5am. I am really bored, I am just lying on my pink, flowery bed, daydreaming, when suddenly my master comes into my bedroom and starts dressing me in pink bows and frills.

My horrid master never lets me go on walks. She says I will get far too dirty, but that is what I want to do. I want to roll about in the mud and get dirty and I want to go on walks. Anyway, instead of all that I have to have four baths a day. The only time I am ever allowed in the lovely outdoors, is when I go to the vets because my master thinks I am critically ill.

My master says today we are having some visitors. The visitors have come to have some tea. When they see me they go mad and start messing with my bows. When they leave, I have to have a horrid bath. I hate baths.

The only good thing about being a poodle is that children like to dress you up and play with you. I do like being played with.

I wish I had a normal life and I wish I was not a poodle anymore. The problem is that I do not have any friends because I never go out so I hardly ever see anyone else but my master!

I get ever so lonely being a poodle.

Hannah Benussi (9)
Fairfield Prep School

A Day In The Life Of A Rabbit

Hello, my name is Arthur Rabbit; it's very gloomy being a rabbit, just sitting here and chewing different types of vegetables.

A couple of hours later, my owner finally lets me out of the cage to explore the garden but sadly I wander off and someone sees me and carries me into their house and puts me in a cage. They start to play with me, *this is all I've ever dreamed of,* I think to myself.

I start to wonder what my real owners are thinking but still this is great, but I just don't want them to find out I am really a human.

I've had a great time with my new owners but I just have to go back to my real ones and this is my plan; when they let me out of my cage in about five minutes time, I will run back to my real owners, that is, if I can find them!

So I am on the way back to my real owner's house - ha, ha there it is! I can recognise that house anywhere because it has moss on the roof.

Oh no, what's happening? I'm changing back. I'm back to being human again. Well what a day in the life of a rabbit that was!

Charlie Richardson (10)
Fairfield Prep School

A Day In The Life Of A Surfboard

Oh no, I'm stranded, great start to the day. I'm getting all wet and I don't like it! This is the second time it has happened this week. Oh dear, I hope I'm imagining it, because I think I can hear the dreaded rumbling of a wave.

Well I wasn't imagining it, wait a minute, I feel very light and it's hard to keep afloat so that must mean . . . I've been split in half by a horrible rock and now I'm really struggling to keep above the water.

Every now and again, I see lots of little fishes and crabs and even the distant sight of a shark, I've been hit once or twice, as I go underwater.

It's started to be a bit calmer now and I'm able to keep myself just about afloat, apart from when I naturally take a look at what's happening beneath me. I'm feeling a bit bored now as there are no waves to take me just a little bit closer to the beach I'm dreaming of being on.

At the start of the day, I didn't want to be alive because I was stranded in the middle of the ocean but now it's simply being bored. Oh hooray, I think I can hear a wave coming. I can, a big one, very big!

After what seemed like hours, I landed next to my other half.

Katarina Jackson (10)
Fairfield Prep School

A Day In The Life Of A Prawn

I wake up in my coral. It is very dark and gloomy, I wonder if the rest of the shoal are awake.

'Mum, Dad are you awake yet?'

'Yes, we're here!' they said sleepily.

I was really hungry so I had some breakfast. It consisted of plankton, plankton and more plankton. It may sound boring but it tastes nice, especially with a cup of sea water.

I could feel it was going to be a busy day because Dad was excited about something.

'Today Son,' he said in his deep voice, 'we are going on an outing.'

First we set out seeing lots of beautiful fish, big ones and small fat ones and thin, pretty ones and ugly ones. Then suddenly as if out of nowhere, came a big great white shark, ten feet long. It snatched a few prawns, so we all darted back to the corals where we hid till the shark had gone back into the darkness.

We carried on looking for any danger. Then for a change we went nearer the surface where there weren't as many predators, or so we thought. Suddenly above us was a black shadow, a net dropped down on the other side of the shoal and the net went back up. Oh no, my friends have gone! We all darted back to the corals. That was the end of a dangerous and busy day.

Sam Bowden (10)
Fairfield Prep School

A DAY IN THE LIFE OF A COIN

At one o'clock in the morning I was put into a purse which smelled sweet and lovely.

Then at eleven o'clock I was taken to the local hat shop where my owner bought a magnificent hat with me. Later on that day, I was sold to a mad scientist who put me under the biggest laser I've ever seen. Then he typed something into a computer next to me. A huge light flashed and I was turned into a pair of shoes! Then the mad scientist sold me to the well-known Bishop of Canterbury.

After this, he sprayed me with some horrid perfume, which smelled of mud but it was a waste of time, because he straight away gave me back to the now sad, mad scientist. Again he put me under a huge laser and turned me back into a coin then threw me out of the window.

Some boys picked me up. They went home to get some glue but they didn't have any glue so they went to the shop with five pounds and bought some glue. They got outside their window and glued me to the pavement then watched people trying to pick me up until nine o'clock!

Edward Hayter (10)
Fairfield Prep School

A Day In The Life Of A Hamster

Yesterday morning I woke up and found out that I was a tiny, fluffy hamster lying on the streets, seeing all the big feet passing me by. I could see cars, buses and lorries all way above me, which was quite strange. I was trying to communicate with people but it was no good, I was too small and too quiet for anyone to hear me.

A girl picked me up and called me Hammy the Hamster. Then she passed me over to her friend who said that I was the cutest thing she had ever seen.

One of the girls, named Kate, said she wanted to take me home and look after me. I wasn't sure about this but I had no choice, so Kate picked me up and took me home to her bungalow, where she put me in a cage with some food, some water and a wheel to run about in.

Suddenly, something weird happened to me, my bones and muscles were getting bigger and bigger. I was transforming back into a human. I quickly stepped out of my cage and I was back to being a human again.

I snuck out of the back door and left Kate and her friend a note to explain what had happened. I doubt they would believe it but I was back to my usual self.

Alex Zaman (10)
Fairfield Prep School

A DAY IN THE LIFE OF A MOUSE

'Aaawww!' I yawned. I scuttled across to my packet of nuts, ten times the size of me. I leapt into the packet and started to nibble savagely at the rock hard, half-eaten nuts.

'Miaow!' cried Morris (the cat who lived in the house). I sprang out of my packet to greet Morris.
Morris however, doesn't chase mice anymore, he's been at my side for seven years and given up the chase now. He's too old I guess!

Thud! Thud! Oh no, it's Michael, the owner of Morris.
As quick as a mouse, I ran through the door, round the corner and through another door and . . . hey, it's my lucky day, in front of me was a slab of chocolate on a metal holder.

As I started to nibble the delicious chocolate. *Splat!* I felt myself rising up - up to Heaven. *A mouse trap!* I should have known. Wheee! This is quite good fun actually. Ow!! I was hit by a jumbo jet, back I fell, back to Earth, right in front of the mousetrap.
'Oh well,' I murmured, 'no more Morris.'
'Miaow!'

Harry Graham (10)
Fairfield Prep School

A DAY IN THE LIFE OF A JEWISH GIRL IN HIDING

As I woke up, Ruth stirred in her sleep. There was not much space in our room and her bed was right next to mine.

I twisted round and looked at the small alarm clock. It was time to get up. Quietly I got up and shook Ruth awake. We tiptoed downstairs from our attic bedroom.

Mama and Papa were already eating and Ruth and I hurried to eat our breakfast.

The day followed its normal pattern: helping Mama with the housework, doing lessons and concocting meals. At the moment our diet is mostly potatoes since that is almost all we can get on the Black Market. Whenever we do anything, we have to be deathly quiet in case anybody hears us. If anybody apart from Margot knew about us, we would be dead.

Margot is the secretary in what used to be my father's business. When Mother was called up and we went into hiding, Margot agreed to help us. Now we rely on her totally.

After supper we gathered round and listened to the news. It's our only contact with the outside world. It seemed that the Germans were doing well and the British had a new Prime Minister.

Suddenly there was a creak from downstairs. Quickly we turned off the radio and Papa crept downstairs to have a look. We should be safe since the door was disguised as a bookshelf. Papa was coming back and with him was Margot. Phew!

Veronica Heney (10)
Fairfield Prep School

A Day In The Life Of An ARP Warden

I woke up with the shivers. At least three bombs had hit Primrose Avenue that night. Last night I'd found an abandoned house, I gathered myself into the house and found a message saying 'Would the Germans have the courage to take over?' I folded the note and put it in my coat. Carefully, I walked away.

I warned everyone about the note. Then I heard the German planes, so I knocked on people's doors to tell them to go to the air raid shelters.

I walked to King's Cross station. The day went quickly and when night-time came, I made sure there was not a peep of light showing.

I found a bottle of cold milk and as I took a sip, I wondered when it was going to be over! Then I heard a bomb drop on the lane where I lived. My mother and children were in the house, I ran to the lane but it was too late, the bomb had demolished our house. There was nothing left but rubble. I felt awful. I walked to the nearest telephone box and phoned Father.

We met together and then went looking in the rubble for the children. We found two dead bodies belonging to the children. Then we found Mother. We both cried our eyes out. From that day I knew it was all over.

Sarina Jassal (10)
Fairfield Prep School

A DAY IN THE LIFE OF A BED

I was in a van being transported from the factory I was born in to somebody's house. I am a four-poster bed and every day my new owner would come and sit on me and start reading a book, then in half an hour, he would close my curtains and go to sleep.

One day the master's son was holding some paint and *splodge* it all came out on me and I was covered in paint. Because my master couldn't get the paint off me I had my legs cut off and that was painful and now I've got new legs. They are made out of pine but I really wanted oak though.

One day I overheard my master talking and he said I am comfy but that I was getting old. To be honest, I didn't actually know how old I was.

It was a normal day, then the dog came under the bed. For a dog it was strong and then it happened, I had been broken. My master came and said goodbye to me. A van came to the front door and then by the time the new bed was probably there, I was being thrown on the dump.

Jaysel Mistry (10)
Fairfield Prep School

A Day In The Life Of A Carrot

'Ouch!' Someone's pulling my hair. The soil around me is collapsing. I had just gotten warm and . . . 'Achoo!'

The air is freezing, it's about minus one. Somebody is taking me out of the garden. I am being swung backwards and forwards.

That's better, I am indoors now. There are more people. They are talking but I don't know what they're saying. I don't understand human language.

'Help!' What is happening? What is that? It's big and shiny and it's coming faster and faster.

'Oh ouch!' That really hurt, what is happening? I think I will roll over and try to stand up. Hold on, where are my feet?'

I did not have time to wonder, the big shiny thing was coming again and again. I was going to die!

Then I was being held over something bubbling. that's nice, it's just like a carrot's dream jacuzzi. Hold on, turn the power down, it's getting too hot. 'Nooo!' I'm being dropped in. I was left there for ages, then the boiling thing, which I had been sitting in, was poured away. I was not sure whether I was alive!

'Yuck!' What's that? It smells, I'll bet it's a smelly cabbage but no, it cannot be, it's all pinky. I know I'll ask it. The reply came in a stealthy voice, 'I'm a pork chop.' That must be the meat but I'm a carrot - a vegetarian.

Francesca Onesti (10)
Fairfield Prep School

A Day In The Life Of An Umbrella

Hi, my name is Alex and I am an umbrella. One day my owner took me out because she was going shopping. My owner, Amelia, took hold of me and stuffed me into her handbag.

The inside of Amelia's handbag was amazing, it was very soft inside and it was warm and it was cosy.

When Amelia and I got outside, she took me from her handbag and held me over her head. Suddenly I felt rain pouring over me. After a while, I got used to the rain, which was now dripping on me. Then something extremely strange happened, Amelia walked into a shop where there were masses of umbrellas, big ones, small ones, medium-sized ones, patterned ones, glittery ones, patchwork ones and loads more.

Amelia walked in front of a mirror to make sure that I had completely shielded her from the rain. I had wondered what I looked like, so I took my chance and looked into the mirror. I was a glittery, denim umbrella but there wasn't much glitter on me and the denim looked very worn. Amelia pushed me into her handbag but this time she did not push me in so far down so I could see the other umbrellas.

Amelia walked towards a stand with lots of umbrellas on. I took one quick glance at them and I spotted one which was just like me. The denim on it was bright and did not look the slightest bit worn and the glitter was scattered over it so that it twinkled in the light. Amelia was going to get a new umbrella. The umbrella and I would be twins.

Saskia Proffitt (10)
Fairfield Prep School

A DAY IN THE LIFE OF A GRANDFATHER CLOCK

Hi, I am a clock. Well not just a clock, I'm a big, old, grandfather clock. All I have been doing for years and years is ticking my way around the clock. Tick, tick, tick, tick, tick! The best thing about being a clock is that lots of people look at you, and it makes you feel so popular. Also when I get my chain pulled it tickles me right over.

I am quite a mad grandfather clock because when I get oiled I drink it all instead, just like a big pint of whisky. It makes me quite dizzy though. It sometimes makes me lose my time but I can't do that I have to hold on to my time! It's very precious. Here it is again, back again to my old ticking because I'm bored. Tick, tick, tick! I live with my owners Beryl and Sid and they have two grandchildren who always like pulling my chains to tickle me.

The house I live in is quite old just like me. I'm eighty-five. Do you know I have my own special key so that no one can open me and mend me if I get ill if they don't have a key. I am starting to get ill quite a lot now because I'm an old fogies. So my owner needs to keep the key safe.

Okay then, I have told you enough now - bye-bye. Tick, tick, tick, tick!

Annie Stanford (10)
Fairfield Prep School

A Day In The Life Of Teddy

Hi! My name is Ted. I am going to tell you how I became who I am.

Today my story begins when I was just one piece of fluffy brown material in a dirty, smelly and shabby factory.

First I was cut up into many different shapes and sizes. Then I was sewn up with stitching, every colour of the rainbow. Before that I was stuffed with white puffy stuff.

Eventually I was thrown into a box with lots of other teddies like myself, but with just one colour of stitching on them. I felt quite special amongst all the other teddies, somehow I thought I was the best ted in the box.

Suddenly I felt the box being lifted into the air. As the box glided somewhere, it became very noisy like a chugg-chugga sound. The noise started getting closer and closer and suddenly I was on the noise and water started seeping through the sides of the box. I was being tossed and turned everywhere.

After about five minutes, the box was full of water. I kicked at the sides of the box making a soggy wet hole. I took a last breath of air and dove into the freezing cold water.

I wriggled through the hole as the box began to sink into the deep shadows, and I swam to the surface of the water.

The next day I found myself in a strangled hug.

Becky Steele (10)
Fairfield Prep School

A Day In The Life Of A Window Cleaner

It's a boring job being a window cleaner. The pay is excellent because I work for the Queen; her house is amazing.

Oh yeah - hi! My name is Steve. Every weekday I clean windows and I get Saturday and Sundays off to spend with my family. My working hours are seven o'clock in the morning until five o'clock at night.

It is very tiring. It takes me two months to clean all the windows. The windows are so big and sometimes I have to hang out of the window to clean them as they are too high for the ladder. Sometimes people passing by, laugh at me and shout horrible things at me like, 'Hi, Mr Window Cleaner, enjoying your smelly, dirty job?'
I just ignore them because I think they are very stupid to say things like that.

The Queen is sometimes very kind to me and she gives me days off work because I work so hard, but that's very rare though. One day she gave me the day off but my wife said that I had to clean our windows and I fell off the ladder and broke my leg.

I had to have ten weeks off and when I got back to work I was so mad because the Queen had paid somebody else my money. I hadn't been given any money for when I was away, even though the Queen promised she would pay me.

Emma Woods (10)
Fairfield Prep School

A Day In the Life Of A Birthday Present

Ouch! This hurts. I'm in the back of a car on the way to a birthday party. Wow! I think, that's the ice rink! It's huge but I hope I'm not going in one of those locker thingies. Uh oh my friends were right, these lockers do smell!

'Hello!' I call. 'Is anyone there?'
I wait - no answer.
All I can hear is people cheering. I wonder if my new master is one of them. I hope so, or that she is nice.

I have been in here for ages but still nobody is coming.

I can hear footsteps, a key in a lock. I wait, nobody comes. It's probably just another locker, I reassure myself. It isn't! I can't believe it, I'm being opened! I'm actually being opened! This is so exciting.

I can see my master now, well mistress then. I'm sitting here on her lap whilst she pretends to feed me her chicken nuggets and strawberry milkshake.

I look around, the ice centre is huge, bigger than any place I've ever seen before in my life. It's amazing! It's like a whole palace full of boys and girls, mums and dads, aunts and uncles! This is the experience of toy-time!

Oh no, she's dropped me and I'm falling to the floor. Bang! Ouch! that hurt. There's a foot coming my way. I'm going to die.

Catriona Davey (10)
Fairfield Prep School

A Day In The Life Of A Cat

'Morning!' Hey why have I got fur? Arggh! I'm a cat. Hopefully this will wear off, this fur's itchy. Oh well, breakfast time I guess. I went and nudged my master.

'Okay Kit-Kat, I'll get you your breakfast.'
I followed him into the kitchen where he got down a bowl with the name Kit-Kat on it. Then he got some food and put it in the bowl and left me alone to eat.

Urrgh! This is disgusting! I'm going to find something better to eat than this stuff. *Cookies!* I couldn't believe it, right there on the top shelf too. Oh I can't reach them. Why me? Why did I have to suffer the pain of being a cat? Hang on a minute, cats can climb. I'm saved!

I leapt up onto the surface and started to get onto my hind legs. Suddenly I leapt high in the air. I soared, I grabbed the cookies between my paws and landed on my feet. Only the packet had been opened and the cookies had scattered everywhere. Oh well, at least I've got the crumbs too! Then my master came in.

'What's going on here? I leave you alone for five minutes and you snap at the cookies!'
'Lunchtime!' called the mistress.

I managed to nap for the rest of the day even if I was stuck outside when it was raining.

Rebecca Holmes (10)
Fairfield Prep School

A DAY IN THE LIFE OF SACHIN TENDULKAR

I woke up one morning and looked in the mirror, I couldn't believe it, I was Sachin Tendulkar, my idol.

I ate my breakfast of Indian food and went in a limousine to meet the Indian team for training. I did a lot of batting practise, some bowling from 10am to 1pm. I had a quick lunch and practised for one more hour before going to the hotel.

I had a long bath so I didn't smell of sweat as I sweated loads.

Dinner was 2 bacon rashers and 2 eggs and 2 slices of toast. We then watched highlights of the last game we played and to see what we could improve on.

There were 6 pool tables so we played pool till 11pm then it was our curfew so we went to bed.

The next day I was back to myself again. *Wow*, I thought, *I want to be just like him.* I'll try to get into the best teams in England or India so I can get into England or the Indian international side when I am 16 years old, in 6 years time.

Dharmist Bathia (10)
Fairfield Prep School

A Day In The Life Of A Frog

I woke that morning to hear a croaky voice calling my name. The voice said, 'Wake up, it's time to go swimming.'
I reluctantly got up and put on my swimming trunks and walked up to the pond with my friend Jon the toad.

The water was warm and we had races between lily pads. Soon we were splashing each other and swimming around.

Meanwhile at the bottom of the pond a pike had spotted us and was about 5 inches away when I spotted the pike. I yelled and we both swam to the bank just in time.

'Come on,' said Jon. 'Let's go and eat some flies. I heard they have really big ones round the corner.'

We ate as many flies as we could, then we got tired and slept for 3 hours.

We woke to find we were lying on a snake, luckily it was still fast asleep so we snuck away. By this time it was dark and soon would be pitch-black.

After a while of wondering around a squirrel came by and said, 'I hope you're not lost. Are you? I'll take you home - I'm going to your house anyway.'

And after that I never slept away from home again.

Matthew Hargrave (10)
Fairfield Prep School

A Day In The Life Of A Fish

I am a purple and yellow rare fish and unfortunately, very tasty to fish-eating enemies. Anyway, yesterday I ran away from home. My mum (I think) doesn't yet know. I'm hoping to find a good home away from predators before tomorrow. I'm just about to explore a house right now!

Oh this is perfect! Just bliss! I'm going to have a little nap.

Five minutes later.

Ouch I'm going! Sorry that was an angry catfish. When I say angry I mean angry. I'm getting away from here.
'I never wanted that house anyway,' I shout obviously lying.

I travel leisurely for about an hour until I meet some luck. Bad luck. Bad luck. It's a hungry, mean-looking shark.
'I'm a little hungry,' he growls.

I'm shivering with fright in a crack in the rock. Suddenly the shark darts forward. I quickly swim down and hide in the seaweed.

The shark knows I'm gone but not where. Rapidly I swim home where I find my mum looking for me as she didn't know I'd gone. I'm glad. I said I'd been for a sleepover with my mate Tom. She was very angry I didn't tell her I was going. Well, she would be wouldn't she?

Sophie Stevens (9)
Fairfield Prep School

A Day In The Life Of A Cuckoo Clock

Hey look at my hands. One is long, one is short and I have got an even longer hand that ticks quite fast. And I have numbers on my face, 1 up to 12.

Oh no, the bird is sleeping, he has got to wake the family up. I will have to tick louder, then the bird will wake the family up. If that does not work then I will have to push the bird into broad daylight and that should wake him up. *Tick-tock.* Oh no, it's not working I will have to push him out, whee, he has woken up.

'Cuckoo!' Yes they are all awake, oh this tick noise is quite annoying. Oh well I will get used to it.

Ting, ting, ting, ting, ting, ting. The clock strikes eight, the children are leaving for school. I am alone, me and the bird who cannot sing. Bird shall I give you some singing lessons? OK let's make a song up, you chirp two times to lead me in . . . oh no it is 6 o'clock, time to go to sleep.

Look I am turning into a human . . .

Sonia Varia (9)
Fairfield Prep School

A DAY IN THE LIFE OF MICHAEL SCHUMACHER

I woke up to find myself in a F1 racing suit. It looked like it was one of my favourite F1 driver's room or somebody who is a big fan of his.

I walked downstairs into his hall, then I walked outside, got in my Ferrari and drove to the racing track and when I got there I was told I had three hours before I was going to race in the F1 Grand Prix in Germany.

I decided to have a practise lap. I got the fastest time out of everybody.

I had a drink then I was called up for my race. I could see the bright red light shining in front of me. The light went amber, get ready, *go!*

I was the fastest off the starting line, but suddenly I had an engine problem, but I got control back. I overtook all of the other racers and I was in the lead. There was a sharp bend coming up, yes I made it round that bend. Right there was just 100 metres to go before the end of the race. *Yes!* I won the race!

I drove home afterwards, had dinner and went to bed.

Ben Addison (10)
Fairfield Prep School

A DAY IN THE LIFE OF MARTIN JOHNSON

6am - I wake up feeling tired. I don't want to get up. The only reason I am getting up so early is because I am sometimes late for training when I wake up at seven. But I think (because I'm so tired) I will get up at seven. So I set my alarm clock for seven, and I go back to sleep.

7am - I wake up again and I have a shower, get dressed and then have my breakfast, get in my car and start driving to the grounds.

8am - I arrived at the grounds 5 minutes ago. I am already in my rugby kit and training's about to start.

8.05am - Training's just started and I've just done a terrific kick . . . I scored a drop goal.

10am - Training is turning out to be a success. We are having a training game in an hour but I'm having a great time.

11am - I'm starting a game now and these are the people on my team: Jonny Wilkinson, Neil Back, Tim Stimpson and a few others.

1pm - Training's going to finish soon, I'm really tired. I wonder what my kids are doing?

4pm - Training's finished now and I'm going home to my loving family.

9pm - I'm home and watching TV. My kids have gone to bed and there's nothing good on TV.

1am - I wake up worrying about the game later . . .

John Portsmouth (9)
Fairfield Prep School

A Day In The Life Of A Slipper

Hi, my name is Mr Slipper and I get worn all the time by my owner. I was waiting for someone to wear me and, well, I was waiting when suddenly I could smell this horrible gas and with great fright a foot came into me and I started to move. First I went into the kitchen and then I had been trodden in dirt. I was all sticky and greasy, and I couldn't move at all. I tried and tried until I finally got pulled out.

Suddenly I got taken off my master's foot and got looked at. I said to myself, 'Now I've got dirt on me my master won't want me anymore.' Then with great shock my master did what I was thinking. He threw me away and never looked at me again.

The next morning I heard the bin men come to collect the rubbish and to take me away. The bin men emptied the rubbish away and suddenly I fell out of the bin. I was resting at the side of the street for hours and hours until I got found.

An old lady found me, took me away and started to clean me. I felt all wet and calm; I thought this lady was really nice to do this.

Soon after I got cleaned up and I was so happy because I was an old pair.

James Ang (10)
Fairfield Prep School

A Day In The Life Of A Key

I woke up after a good night's sleep, suddenly my master picked me up, pushed me in the keyhole, turned my handle and opened the door. If this is what being a key is like I don't want to be one. It's very dark in this keyhole, my master then shut the door, turned me again and pushed me through the letterbox and I landed on the soft, furry carpet.

Then my master's wife picked me up, put me on the table and went to cook breakfast. James had just woken up, then he got ready and said, 'Mum, I'm going to my friend's house.'
His mother replied, 'Eat your breakfast first James.'
So he went to eat his breakfast.

Then he came back, put me in the dark keyhole, opened the door, went out, shut the door, turned me and locked the door.

He put me in his pocket when suddenly I fell out. I lay there on the cold, rough floor. Then my master's wife took a key out of her pocket, it's my brother, he is in a lot of pain because his handle is broken. She then went out.

After a while a man dressed in all-black clothes picked me up, put me in the keyhole, opened the door, then he came out with a bag full of things. Soon I noticed everything in the house had been stolen. Who would do such a thing?

Karan Bhardwaj (10)
Fairfield Prep School

A DAY IN THE LIFE OF A CAT

My name is Amber. Yesterday was a terrible day. My sister Alice got hit by a car. My owners are being very nice to me. They don't normally pay much attention to me, but today they're being extremely kind. All this attention is getting a bit too much. I think I'll go out for a bit. But where shall I go? I think I might go to the allotments where Alice was found.

Oh no, It's raining, I'd better go back home. Yoww! It's hailing. I'll have to hurry up. Oh piddles, the cat flap's blocked. I try scratching on the door but they can't hear me. Where can I shelter? I'll try down the side of the garage, even though it's a terrible squash. It's very uncomfortable but at least I haven't got hailstones hitting my head.

It's getting very cold and I'm getting hungry. I'm going to venture out. Yoww! It's snowing. I retreat back down the side of the garage. I'm getting sleepy. I wish I was on top of the boiler.

'Amber, Amber, where are you?' the calls cut into my dreams. I give a small miaow. The footsteps are getting closer. 'Amber, are you there?' I give another miaow. A hand appears. I stand up and nudge the hand. The hand pulls me out and hugs me. I'm wrapped in a warm blanket and taken inside. A bowl of milk is put in front of me. I lap it up. I'm safe at home, safe and sound.

Jessica Aryeetey (10)
Fairfield Prep School

A DAY IN THE LIFE OF A LUCKY CHARM

I woke up to see the usual red velvet that keeps me warm during the cold winters. The lid opened letting in a stream of beautiful light, my mistress' hand reached in and pulled me up. I went in a warm pocket and was buttoned in.

I fell asleep until I was pulled out and placed on a wooden desk. I realised my mistress had a test, I hope I give her enough luck. She slipped me gently onto her wrist. It was warm and cosy, like the cloth in my box. I was happy to give her lots of luck, she did treat me kindly after all. My blue velvet rubbed on her wrist as she wrote the story. I caught a glimpse of it. It seemed very good.

I was taken off at the sound of the lunch bell and the papers were handed in. I was back in the warmth of my mistress' blazer pocket, it was good, it was buttoned up as I jogged up and down on the journey home.

A couple of hours later I was back, comfortably, in my own box, my own red box, not many bracelets get that kind of treatment! I am happy to be my mistress' lucky charm, she does take good care of me, so I give her lots of luck. I am her favourite thing and I hope I always will be.

I will be happy when she gets her mark back, as I am sure (with my luck) she will get a good one.

Charlotte Aspinall (10)
Fairfield Prep School

A DAY IN THE LIFE OF A RICH PRINCESS

I woke up in the morning looking at my wonderful rich bedroom. It was a lovely cream bedroom which was very bright and spacious. Outside the birds chirped and sang a musical song. My bed had a big canopy over my headboard. It was a lovely day outside. I drew my curtains and outside I saw an enormous garden. I then decided to go to breakfast.

Breakfast was sausages, baked beans, a fried egg, orange juice, Rice Krispies, melon and grapes. What a spread. When I was extremely full I ran to our own swimming pool. I had a swim in the warm water and then I decided to go to the beach.

The sand tickled my feet as I walked along. I made sandcastles and then went in the water. It was luke warm and the waves came to greet me. In the distance I could see a speedboat coming towards me. It was now coming quite close and was just about to go on top of me. So I quickly ran back home.

The servants at the great palace were busy making all kinds of food. They brought me some tea and cakes and I politely accepted it. I told my servants that I was going out shopping now.

I found a lovely pearl dress and it was quite cheap for me. It was £3,000. I thought I would buy it, but it was the last one and it was saved. So I went back home very disappointed.

Saira Badiani (10)
Fairfield Prep School

A Day In The Life Of Ashley Olson (From 2 Of A Kind)

It is the first day of the term, the bell went 5 minutes ago so I'm late for class already. It is a great start to the day! First I get told off on the bus and now I'm late for class. Well when I get to class I really get told off and my sister Mary-Kate Olson has saved me a seat.

The first lesson is maths, boring maths. Maths is the most boring, boring, boring lesson. Next lesson is English, then science, then PE, then lunch.

After lunch we have ICT, then art, then double French, then library.

We start school at 8.30am and finish at 4pm.

We have walkie-talkies when we wash up. We are identical twins so we've got the same clothes on and the same beds. We have the same teacher, the same lessons, the same posters, you get the idea. We both hate maths and both love PE and ICT. Music is our favourite subject because we love dancing and we go dancing and horse riding. We like football as well, but best of all we are twins all day!

Hannah Baxter (10)
Fairfield Prep School

A Day In The Life Of A Kettle

Hi, I'm a kettle, I call myself Freddie because the shop I came from was called Freddie's Kitchen-Use Store. My master is Mr T Dulac, he works in the skateboarding industry. The mistress is Mrs H Dulac, she is kind and on Friday evenings she makes Mr T Dulac his favourite pie which is peach and plum pie.

In the mornings Mrs H Dulac makes tea for herself and Mr T Dulac. As she pours the water into my stomach I begin to warm up. Then after a few minutes she picks me up by my dark green handle and pours all my warm contents into a teapot which has the tea bags in.

My master and mistress are very kind to me because they let me call them by their first names, which are Tom and Helen.

My day consists of making tea at 11 o'clock for Tom and Helen. At half-past 11 Tom goes to work in Cambridge, at his store. They sell decks, tricks, wheels, fully-made boards, clothing and skateboarding equipment.

At 2 o'clock Tom shuts up the shop for ten minutes while he eats his lunch. His lunch consists of jam sandwiches and a Golden Delicious apple, and then he stops the shop until 8 o'clock which is when he closes the shop and goes home for dinner.

When Tom gets home dinner is on the table. He sits down at the end of the polished pine table. He looks down at the table and he sees bowls and plates full of honeybee soup for starters and for the main course he has roast chicken, boiled potatoes and vegetables. For a drink he has a selection of vintage wines and for dessert he has plum and peach pie with ice cream, also with a cup of strong tea, and that's average Friday.

William Bourne (9)
Fairfield Prep School

A Day In The Life Of A Handkerchief

I am a handkerchief, I am red and silky. At the moment I am in a pitch-black shut drawer. Now someone is opening the cupboard and reaching in to get something and it's me. I wonder what things will happen to me today.

He is putting me in his black blazer pocket. Now he is reaching to get me and he is unrolling me and all this liquid green stuff is coming on to me. I think it is snot. Now he is putting me back in his blazer pocket.

It will take quite a long time to get rid of all this snot, but what's worse is it really stinks. I am starting to dry off. Oh no, he's taking me out again, but now we are at home and yes he is throwing me in the washing machine. I like them because they make me dizzy.

I was enjoying myself when it stopped and somebody else, a woman, picked me up and put me in the dryer. I love this it's so warm and comfortable. I was in here for about 30 minutes, when I get out I am all crinkly.

Now I am going to board with a blue cover it is an ironing board. I am getting less creased every second and then she stops. I am all straight and felt brilliant. I am being folded up and put in the same wooden cupboard, then I go to noddy land.

Nayan Chauhan (10)
Fairfield Prep School

A Day In The Life Of Harry The Dog

Slobber, slobber, wag, wag, good morning everyone, *woof, woof, smile, wag, wag.* I am Harry the black lab. My favourite thing to do is eat lots and lots.

Today my mission is to steal that pound of butter off the side and maybe that big, juicy apple in the fruit bowl, that certainly stands out.

It is breakfast time now . . . gone already, *lick, lick.* Down come the children (this means second breakfast, *yum, yum*). My crafty trick always works. It's easy really, all you do is wait till someone is lifting their yummy grub to their mouth and then when it is halfway there . . . *yum, yum,* it's mine! Oooh dear! What have I done wrong? I have been told off and sent to bed. I try howling but no answer. I howl again, it works but in the wrong sort of way.
'Harry, shut up!'

Phew! By lunchtime I am friends again. This time another trick is needed. This is a bit harder but works quite well. What you do is lie low to the ground, then do an army commando move to the table. Next you need to do snake head and long tongue . . .

Whoopee! My second mission completed. I am sent to bed again.

My last mission is easy because all I do is jump up . . . *snap, snap, crunch, gone!* I have an early night and in a few minutes I am fast asleep and snoring.

Twelve hours later . . . *slobber, slobber, wag, wag,* good morning everyone!

Georgina Armour (10)
Fairfield Prep School

BUSTED'S DAY

It's a normal day for me! Ooh hello I didn't see you there, I'm Mathew
- *whoa!*

Where am I? Hey there's Busted, I think I am in a time wall! I am, hey
I've seen a glimpse of them getting on a blue bus. I'm following it.

Hey, they've stopped at the Albert Hall, they're going in, it's a concert.

2 hours go by.

Wow! Two hours of Busted performing!

Off the bus. We're at BBC Radio 5 Live studios, I can hear them.

30 Minutes go by.

Off we go.

Hey we're at Buckingham Palace and I've been invited to a party.

3½ hours go by.

I've been to the party of my life, it was excellent.

Off we go again. We're at HMV, they've just released a new single
called 'You Said No'.

We go following the bus again. It's like the Wizard of Oz.
Now we're at BBC Radio 3. It's another half hour interview.

We go again, now we're at a secret location. It's a hour long press
conference.

It's 8pm, nearly my bedtime! I'm just in time for tea and what an action
packed day for me, but guess what I got? Busted's autographs, yippee!

At last I've what I've always wanted and I've been to Buckingham
Palace, and I met the Queen. Well it's only five minutes till my
bedtime, so I've gotta go!

Mathew Davies (8)
Greenfields Primary School

THE BOY AND THE HAUNTED HOUSE

Once upon a time there was a little boy called Thomas, he was a kind little boy, always doing things for other people, like helping old ladies cross the road, that's how nice he was.

One day he went to the haunted house and it was really scary in there for him. There was a big, frightening monster who chased him, along with some other horrible monsters. Thomas was really scared, he didn't know what to do, thankfully his friends Rhian, Matthew, Lily, Amy and Zoë were with him. They were really scared too, they decided to run away from the monsters.

They ran as fast as they could and entered a bedroom. Inside the room were lots of little beds, then suddenly a witch appeared and they shook with fright.
'A witch!' cried Thomas.
'What are we going to do?' said Amy.
'It's OK, she's a friendly witch, she will help us escape,' Matthew replied.
'That's correct my pretty, quick, get on my broomstick and we can fly out of the window,' the witch commanded.

The children climbed onto the witch's broomstick and just then the monsters broke down the bedroom door and ran at them. 'Help!' they wailed.
'Go!' screamed Zoë and with a whoosh the witch carried away the children on her broomstick, out through the window and into the night.
'Where do you want to go?' asked the witch.
'Back to Greenfield's School to tell Miss French about our adventure,' Rhian replied.
'She will never believe us!' sighed Lily.

Ella Preece (8)
Greenfields Primary School

THE EVIL EVENT

'Amy stop balancing with your left foot on the floor.'
Today was balancing day at West Harlscott Junior School and everyone in class 4b had to balance on a long rope above a bendy blue mat and Mrs Strict, the class teacher, was poking them in the back to make them go faster.
'William!' called Mrs Strict in a loud voice, 'get on this rope immediately!'
Weak William climbed onto the rope and walked slowly towards the end.
'Hurry up!' screamed the teacher and gave William a huge push. William fell off the rope and landed on the mat. No sooner had William fell on the mat he had fallen down a deep hole.
'Amy, try again and do it right!'
Amy climbed onto the rope and jumped off, Bethany did the same.
'Arrrghh!' they screamed as they fell down the hole.

Please be a soft landing, they thought, to their surprise it was. They had landed on a pile of witches' hats. They looked around and saw a small black figure staring at them.
'Ah hah!' the figure said. 'I was wondering when I would be able to trap you.'
Bethany and Amy took a few steps back.
'My name is Anna the Ache and I am a witch, come and meet my daughter,' said the witch.
She showed them a small vampire. 'My name is Danielle the Disaster and I shall show you to your cage.'

Danielle showed them a huge cage and before they could say, 'What an evil event,' they were pushed straight into the cage.
'What do we do now?' whispered Amy.
Bethany turned around and said, 'I've found a door and it might lead to where the Devil lives.'

'What devil?' said Amy in a worried voice.
'The Devil who trapped William,' replied Bethany.

They opened the door slowly and walked inside. What they saw was terrifying. In the corner of the room they saw the Devil. They ran up and stabbed him with a horn that they had found on the floor. They found a key in the Devil's ear and unlocked William. It had been a tiring day, but they still had the trip back . . .

Emily Smith (8)
Greenfields Primary School

VAMPIRE VILLE

Long, long ago in a vampire world, there lived the red crystal of birth. Whenever it shone brightly it was always a sign of a new vampire being born. It was shining ever so brightly, just like a red sun blazing in the distance.

This was no ordinary vampire, it was the demon vampire they all had been waiting for. Sneakily someone didn't obey the great master, so he didn't trust any of the others and he made them all disappear, no one has seen a single vampire since.

'Right,' said the teacher, who was telling the story as the school bell rang, 'bye children, have a happy Hallowe'en.'
'I hate Hallowe'en, it's stupid,' shouted the little boy. He was going on holiday. He was going to where the vampires had been vanished from. The boy had a very rare disease, it was something to do with his blood and heart. The boy cycled home from school, in a very grumpy mood, to get ready for his holiday.

'We are here now,' called his mum.
'So!' the boy mumbled.
'It's your bedtime,' Mum told him.

The wind was creeping higher and higher. Suddenly it was time for the demon vampire to arrive. He drank the boy's blood and the vampire died because of the boy's rare disease.

Luke, the boy, got all the vampire's energy and didn't die. When he got home he told all of his friends about the vampire.

Bethany de Max (8)
Greenfields Primary School

THE ADVENTURE IN THE JUNGLE

There once were two boys named Matt and James and they went camping for two days. They had to get up very early in the morning to get their stuff and go camping in the jungle. When they went out of the front door it was dark and there was something mysterious going on, so they went to find out what. They saw pirates and they were heading into the jungle.

The next day Matt and James went to find the pirates and they found treasure, but the pirates saw Matt and James, so they climbed the tree. When they got to the top there was a snake, they were trapped. They shouted, 'Help!'

The pirates were cutting the tree down. There were two branches tied together so Matt and James went to climb the other tree and they got there eventually. The tree fell on top of the pirates and they were killed.

The next day, when Matt and James woke up, Matt, said, 'I am glad that the pirates are dead. We should have a little walk before we go.'

Then they had to pack. When they had finished packing, they went home. They told Mum about the adventure.
Mum said, 'You had an exciting time!'

After they had their tea and watched the television, they went to bed and so did Mum. They kept talking and Mum said, 'Shhh!' and so they fell asleep.

Sarah Pryce (8)
Greenfields Primary School

ZOMBIES AND WITCHES HA HA HA!

Once upon a time there was a girl called Pop and a boy called Bubbles. They went to their dad's funeral. The only problem was that they got lost and couldn't find their way back. By the time they got back everyone had gone. Probably because it was eleven o'clock at night. It seemed a bit spooky, something wasn't quite right.

Then Bubbles and Pop heard a creak! 'What was that noise Bubbles?'
'I don't know!'
'Shall we go and have a look?'
'OK.'
And there was a zombie. 'Is it Dad?'
'Yes it is.'

Then there was a *bang!* They were inside a coffin, it was dark, wet, spooky and there were lots of hairy spiders. It was gruesome. Then Bubbles and Pop heard a 'Ha ha ha!' It was a witch and a zombie.
'What are we going to do?'
'We should be OK in here.'
Creak! The coffin opened, the zombie and witch were still in the same place. They held their breath, counted to three and ran.

The next day Bubbles and Pop realised that it was all a silly little dream.

Amy Kennelly (8)
Greenfields Primary School

THE HUNGRY WEREWOLF

Once upon a time there lived a boy called John and a girl called, Nittasha. They were both playing on their computer game 'Doomsville' when a hand came and took them right in the game.
'Where are we?' said Nittasha.
'We are . . . are in our game,' said John.

Then a werewolf came out. He came over to them. He said, 'I will rip your heads off and eat you.'
John tried to think of a plan, then he had it. 'Why don't I go and look for a door to escape?'
'Okay,' said Nittasha.

John was looking for hours for a door to escape through. He looked for at least 50 shops.

He was so tired when he suddenly saw a hotel, but then he thought about Nittasha. He ran back as fast as he could to the werewolf's cave. He saw the werewolf looking for his cook book. John quickly snuck Nittasha out of the cave but it got worse, the werewolf had heard them. He came running after them. The werewolf fell over just as John found a door. He opened it and they ran through. The werewolf was still running after them so John locked it.

George Dourish (8)
Greenfields Primary School

THE HAUNTED DREAM

There was once a boy called Jimmy and a girl called Ella. It was their mum and dad's wedding.

Ella and Jimmy went for a walk in the wood. They saw a house and knocked on the door. It opened on its own. Ella went in first, she shouted Jimmy. Jimmy went in.
'Don't be a baby!' said Ella.
'I am not,' said Jimmy.
'There, there, there!' said Ella.
'Look! There's a ghost,' gasped Jimmy.
'There's no such thing as ghosts,' said Ella.
'Ohhhh!'
Ella turned around, 'Stop that noise. I know that you are pretending!'
'No, it's not me!'
'Yes it is!'
'Look there's a ghost, I meant it! Argh, there's a ghost!'
They went through the door that was open. They jumped in. It lead them to more ghosts in ghostland.

At home their mum and dad were wondering where they had got to. They were getting ready for the wedding.

Ella and Jimmy were scared, all the ghosts were scaring them.
'Stop it!' shouted Ella.
'Stop being a baby!'
'I am not!' shouted Jimmy. 'I am just younger than you and I am really scared, we should be at home getting ready for Mum and Dad's wedding, oh why did we go for a walk?'

'Ella started to cry, 'I really wanted to be Mum's bridesmaid. She's got me a lovely dress.'

The room they were in grew dark and menacing. They could feel the evil even if they could not see it.

It was closing in all around them. Ella and Jimmy held each other tight, Ella closed her eyes and thought they were going to die.

'Ella! Ella! Come on, this is the last time I am going to call you. Your bridesmaid dress is all ready for you. *Get up now!*'

Rhian Jones (9)
Greenfields Primary School

THE BLOOD-SUCKING BEAST

One spooky night Barry and Brittany went for a walk through the woods, going past very old, smelly oak trees. At the very moment they saw a spooky, damp, smelly cave.
Brittany said, 'Let's go in.'
So they both went into the cave.

As they walked in the smell made them feel sick. Brittany saw something from the corner of her eye, as she tried to focus Barry let out a loud, chilling scream. The floor started to move, the walls were dripping with red jelly-like slime. As they looked at the floor it was not that that was moving, but the big black creatures. The sound of them moving, crushing each other as they tried to get to Barry and Brittany.

The two began to run deeper into the cave, but they had a big mistake, they should have ran out of the cave. As they got deeper into the cave everything went quiet. They could not see in front, or behind them.

Both of them were shaking, fear running deep into their blood. As they walked they both felt like someone was following them. They turned quickly. To their horror they saw the blood-drenched beast. His fangs were dripping with what looked like blood. He was looking for more food. His big red eyes glowing at the thought of food.

All that could be heard in the dark, smelly cave was the crunching of *bones.*

Jiyan Kutlay (9)
Greenfields Primary School

A Day In The Life Of Rachel Edwards

One day Rachel was on tour, when she realised that she was on in one minute. She rushed to do her make-up. She ran to the stage looking like a clown. She looked at Jo, and Jo laughed at her. Rachel's boyfriend was in the crowd and he saw her face. He jumped up onto the stage and Rachel ran off. He started dancing and he was pretty good.

Rachel sat down and started crying. S Club 7 had to do their next song, but Jon stayed off to find Rachel. He found Rachel and told her it didn't matter and that they all liked her.
'Do you?'
Well, Rachel walked out of the room sulking quietly. She walked back to the stage. Everybody, including the grans and grandads smiled. Jo said sorry.

They finished the tour and Jo said to Rachel, 'It's not that bad.'
'It's happened to us,' said Tina and Bradley.
'Oh. You've forgotten it's my birthday.'
'No we haven't it's the 9th April.'
'It is the 9th April!'
'I'm just going to the shop,' said the rest of S Club 7.
'I never forgot your birthday,' said Jeremy. 'Here is your present.'
It was a cute Labrador. It jumped out of the box and rubbed his head against Rachel's leg.
'Ah,' said Rachel.
Paul picked the Labrador up and Rachel said thanks.
'I bought you a top,' said Jo.
'We bought you chocolates,' said the rest of S Club 7.
And she lived happily ever after.

Lily Jones (8)
Greenfields Primary School

HAUNTING HORRORS

One Friday night Harry Haunting was going trick or treating, when suddenly lightning struck. Harry was terrified of lightning. There was going to be a thunderstorm.

He ran to knock on a door, an old lady dressed up as a witch came to the door, gave him some sweets and said, 'You should go back home, I've just seen the news. It said all children must go inside. There's a murderer around.'
Harry said, 'I live streets away and I'm lost.'
'Well do you want to come in and phone your mum to come and take you home?'
'Yes please!' said Harry, quivering with fear.

Harry dialled his mum's number, someone answered, *'Hello this is your worst nightmare speaking!'*

Harry slammed down the phone and walked into the old lady's living room shivering as he went. He saw the old lady just putting down the phone.
She said, 'Now you know how it feels to have someone play a prank on you! It was me and your family that arranged everything, the thunderstorm was just luck though! Happy Hallowe'en!'

Debbie Reeve (11)
Humberstone Junior School

A Day In The Life Of An Animal

One hot day I was going to the park with all of my friends until we saw this house.

'Shall we go?' said Jack.

All of his friends were all up for it.

Jack walked up to the door, his friends stayed behind. 'I am not scared you donkeys! I know you wouldn't go in but I'm still going.'

So Jack went in. There was a sign saying *Twenty-five stairs to climb.*

So Jack went up, '1, 2, 3, 4, 5, 6, 7, 8, 9, 10, 11, 12, 13, 14, 15, 16, 17, 18, 19, 20, 21, 22, 23, 24, 25. Right that's all the stairs.' So Jack walked through a doorway and there was a strange, mysterious-looking man sitting on a sofa.

The man looked at Jack, 'What do you want my child?' said this man.

'Can you change me in to a dog?' said Jack.

'Yes,' said the man.

1, 2, 3, puff.

Jack turned into a dog and he ran up to the front door and the man let him out.

Jack got taken by the dog keeper and put in the kennels. He was put in room five but he dug a hole out and he ran to the house to ask the man to change him back.

'Change me back!' said Jack.

'OK. 1, 2, 3 - back to normal!'

And Jack learned to not be so selfish and so they lived happily ever after.

Aimee Thompson (11)
Humberstone Junior School

THE ABANDONED HOUSE

On one hot sunny day, four people were playing rounders in a meadow. Their names were: Anthony, Emma, Liam and Kate. After playing for ten minutes Liam hit the ball into a shadowy patch of land. Anthony went to fetch the ball.

When he found the ball he was standing in front of a big, old house so he quickly called the others and went inside.

When the others stepped into the house, Anthony looked up the staircase and saw two silvery figures, it freaked them out so they went back home.

When they came to their street they spotted an old man.
'Hello,' he said, 'you must be the ones to solve why the Riddle family abandoned the old house,' he said softly.
The group just walked away.

The next day they went back to the house, looked back up the staircase and saw a woman holding two children being held by the scruff of their necks. Kate took an ornament off a table beside her and ran up the staircase and shouted at the woman. She threw the object with all her might, but it went straight through the woman and she vanished. Kate looked puzzled and went to the children.
'Are you alright?' she asked them, but they vanished too with nothing more than a whispered, 'Thank you.'
Kate smiled and the group decided to go home and never went there again.

Chay Carter (11)
Humberstone Junior School

A DAY IN THE LIFE OF A CATERPILLAR!

It was that time of day I hated, maths. Maths is bad enough but we had fractions! I gazed out of the window and saw a caterpillar.

Then I began to wonder what it would be like to be a caterpillar, it would be really cool! I could: sleep, wake up and eat, well OK I could get used to the whole eating leaves thing. (Oh to be a caterpillar!)

I don't know how long I was thinking for, but all I knew was this daze became a deep daydream.

Was I? *No! Yes!* I was a caterpillar. *Oh the fun I could have,* I thought, sliding up and down huge, tall poles. *Ahh!* A thrush, my science days had paid off! I crawled, my legs moved faster than any other caterpillar! I then found . . . a chrysalis emerging round me. I fell asleep.

'Lauren, Lauren! Can you pass me the rubber?'
I then came back to reality . . . but you must admit, it was a good daydream!

Lauren Rees (11)
Humberstone Junior School

A DAY IN THE LIFE OF CHAY

One dark, chilly morning a dangerous, wild lion was chasing me up and down the street. I finally jumped into the river and swam to the other side. I was safe there because there wasn't a bridge for two miles.

I ran home and told my mum about it all. She wasn't surprised because it had all happened to her at the supermarket.

At school the lion had cornered a child called Adam. I broke a plank of wood off the balcony and hit the lion around the back. All the children were throwing pebbles at the lion. I threw a brick next to the lion and the balcony fell through. The lion was trapped, I phoned the lion squad and we all lived happily ever after.

Jamie McPhee (10)
Humberstone Junior School

THE ADVENTURE

One sunny afternoon there were seven children. Their names were Katie, Katie, Rachael, Sophie, Robert, Kelly and Matthew. The girls had plaits in their hair. The boys had spiky hair.

They all had pets. Sophie had a dog. Katie had a fish. Kelly had a hamster. Matthew had a guinea pig. Katie had a cat. Rachael had a horse. Robert had a rabbit.

They had a magic key. Every time it glowed it would lead to an adventure. The magic key glowed and it took them to a zoo. There were loads of animals there. There was a lion, sand cat, seals, monkeys and loads of other things. All the children said, 'I love the animals.' Then the children said to the man who worked there, 'Would you feed them so we can watch?'
The man said, 'Of course I will!' so he fed them some meat.

One of the lions escaped. All the children ran. The man tried to catch the lion. He caught it with a big net. Then their adventure ended.

Sophie Greenwood (10)
Humberstone Junior School

A Day In The Life Of Sophie The Witch

Sophie had a black cat, a spider and a bat. She went out at night on her broom and changed anything she didn't like. Sophie enjoyed being a witch, she loved to go out at night. Her pets enjoyed being with Sophie. She fed her pets mashed potatoes and porridge. But her bat ate steak.

One night Sophie flew with her pets, they were riding on Sophie's crooked broom. Suddenly Sophie's broom snapped. Sophie and her pets fell down, her cauldron got caught on a branch of a tree.

Sophie and her pets landed in the cauldron and the branch snapped, sending her cauldron crashing to the ground.

Sophie didn't need to use magic because she had been flung out of her cauldron already. Sophie's pets landed on a pile of red, yellow, brown and green leaves.

Sophie helped herself up. She took her pets inside and they went straight to bed. Sophie's bed was a four-poster so her pets slept there too.

Matthew Smith (11)
Humberstone Junior School

MURDERED TIMMY

One dark afternoon Timmy's mum called him. She asked if he could go to the farm and get some eggs. His mum gave him £5. As Timmy was walking down the street he bumped into his friends. They asked him if he wanted to go to the arcade and he said yes.

When Timmy walked out of the arcade he only had £1 left. He walked to the farm, he asked the farmer for a box of eggs and the farmer asked for £1.50. Timmy was in trouble.

Timmy asked the farmer if he had a smaller box for £1. The farmer gave Timmy two eggs. Timmy walked to the graveyard and sat next to his grandad's grave. When he got up the gate was next to a very large grave, the grave opened and Timmy ran home screaming.

When he got home he put the eggs on the table and said goodnight to his mum. That night when everyone was asleep Timmy needed the loo so he went to the bathroom. When he finished he walked out of the bathroom and there was a pair of red eyes in front of him. Timmy ran to bed.

In the morning Timmy's mum went into his room and his head was in his hand, his belly was chopped open and his insides were hanging out. Timmy had been murdered.

Victoria Lee (11)
Humberstone Junior School

A DAY IN THE LIFE OF SANTA CLAUS

Santa had just returned to the North Pole from Starbucks Café. 'Load me up!' For next week was Christmas, but today was his birthday, he was 3051 so he had a *big cake!* It covered a radius of 6,000 square miles.

Santa just jumped straight into the cake but the candles were not put out so . . . 'Ouch it burns!'
'It's going to Santa,' said one of the elves. 'Let's get you to the hospital.'
'Oh ah, it stings.'
'Here's a cup of cocoa. Now go to sleep. We'll sort out everything for Christmas!'

Hardeep Rai (11)
Humberstone Junior School

THE CREEPY HOUSE

One summer's day Emma and her best friend Katy were walking home from school,
'Do you want to go to the park afterwards?' gasped Katy.
'Yes, but first I'll ask my mum,' said Emma.
'Oh Katy don't forget to bring water before you get dehydrated,' Emma said, while wondering what would happen.
'OK, bye.'

Emma went home. 'Mum! I'm home, she yelled. 'Mum!' she screamed. She went to have a glass of water and there was a note on the fridge. It said, 'I'll be home at six. Gone to town with Katy's mum xxx'.

Emma quickly rang Katy, 'Hi Katy it's me, Emma.'
'Oh, hi. I don't know where my mum is!'
'She's gone to town with my mum.'
'Oh.'
'Do you want to go to the park?'
'Yes.'
'Meet you there, bye.' Emma put the phone down.

Emma rushed to get there fast. Katy was there before Emma.
'Katy, what is in that rucksack?'
'Food!'
'Oh.'
They started walking. They were near the creepy house.
'Hey do you want to go inside and see if the story's true?'
'What story?'
'You don't know the story about why this is a creepy house?'
'Oh, that story.'
'So do you want to go in?'
Katy never answered.

They went in, the door creaked and they stepped back. They fell into a black hole. Find out what happens next . . . in the creepy house!

Bilkis Ebrahim Patel (11)
Humberstone Junior School

THE LOCKET SPIRITS

Ding-dong (doorbell)
'Trick or treat?'
'Oh hi Kate,'
'Hi Max!'
'I'll just get my coat.'
'Max, let's go to that towerhouse. It looks really spooky.'
'OK.'

Ding-dong (ehrrr . . .) The door opened.
'Hello anyone here?'
All of a sudden the towerhouse began to shake. Kate and Max hid behind a curtain, then red smoke began to appear.

'Ahh soon I shall be the most powerful witch in the world!' the witch cried in her screechy voice. 'All human spirits shall be trapped in this locket and all I have to do is read this spell.'
'But your evilness, what if someone finds the golden locket? They could release everyone's spirits!'
'But we'll find it first, Mildred and I don't want your opinion thank you! Ahha!'
'Kate we've got to find that golden locket!'

'In two hours, when the moon rises, I shall be the most powerful witch in the world!'

Find out what happens next in the second book . . . The Chase!

Anjali Patel (11)
Humberstone Junior School

THE DIARY OF DESTINY

January 1st - Starting new diary that I got for Christmas. A new girl has moved in next door and she's blonde. I wish I was blonde. It's not fair. She is really pretty as well.

January 2nd - I've tried making friends with her, she laughed at some of my jokes. I've told her my name's Sinead but she just said 'Nice.' I think she likes me now.

January 3rd - Last night it was great. She called for me and introduced me to the gang and to the den. It's great, she gave me a nickname, Naddy.

January 6th - I'm having the time of my life. Sometimes the gang's not there so it's just me and Nita. We talk about loads of things, especially boys. I helped decorate the den a bit more.

January 7th - I can't believe it, Nita's got a boyfriend and left me in the lurch. She doesn't hang around with us anymore.

January 10th - It was our exam yesterday and I have revised a lot so I found it easy, but I let Nita copy because if I didn't she wouldn't be my friend. She only copied a bit, anyway she was nice to me.

January 15th - I can't believe it, Nita has skanked me now that she's got a 'B' (her highest score). I thought she was a true friend, but now I guess I know! I was so stupid letting her copy me.

January 20th - I've cried every night so far and now I've found a solution - to show this diary, maybe she'll know what she's done to me.

February 1st - She read my diary, gave it back without saying a word, all I know is she moved away yesterday. Who knows what she thinks of me now? But I miss her.

Adella Mulla (11)
Humberstone Junior School

A DAY IN THE LIFE OF A DOG

One summer's day, I was walking down to the beach when my owner was shouting at me loudly. As far as I knew I hadn't done anything wrong. He started tugging me and pulling me, so I bit the inside of his leg and wriggled out of my lead. I was so happy, for all those years I had been beaten.

I was free. I had been running for hours. Finally I was away from him. So I stopped running. I was so hungry. All of a sudden a girl walked in front of me. She said, 'Hello there!'
I laid down and rolled over, I thought she was going to hurt me. I heard her say to her mother standing behind her, 'Can we keep her? Can we?'
Her mother said, 'Well . . . OK then but on one condition. You have to be really good and look after her.'

I had a home finally. So they took me home and they put me in a basket. I lived so, so happily. That was the end of my journey. Finally I had found a home.

Leah Griffin (11)
Humberstone Junior School

THE GHOST OF 1773

In an old haunted house on the top of Bowhill began the story of ghost Gansur the gardener. In 1773 he and his beautiful wife lived in the house. Of course in that year it wasn't a haunted house, at least they didn't think so.

One night he said to his wife, 'I'm off to bed. I'll see you in a moment.' His wife Victoria replied, 'I'll be up in a minute anyway.'

Gansur stumbled up the stairs while Victoria locked the doors. Then Victoria walked slowly up the stairs and towards the bedroom door. She began to open the door . . . she pushed the door open. 'Argh!' screamed Victoria frantically as she stumbled closer. She saw her husband lying dead across the bed. He had an old rusty kitchen knife in his back and gardening worms crawling in his wounds.

She ran screaming down the stairs, she fell to the ground with a knife in her back. They both laid dead in the house and they still lie there today. No one has ever been there since. Do *you* know who did it? I do . . .

Lucy Gamble (11)
Humberstone Junior School

SPOOKS

I had never been more scared in my life, the creature had bloodstained robes, sharp fangs and eyes that would scare anyone to death.

Wait a minute I really should tell you how I got here. It all started last week when I entered the legendary haunted house.

Me, Lynzy and my best mate Kelly had been interested in haunted houses and ghosts for ages, and last week we plucked up the courage to enter Winsted Manor.

It was midnight when we entered the house. When the sky was clear, when the moon was full and when the werewolves began to howl.

We walked into a shabby living room and there was a fireplace with markings around it. I went to examine it. 'Ch-ch-chains,' stuttered Kelly. She was right, there were chains either end of the room. I looked behind Kelly. *'Monster!'* I yelled.
Thud . . . blackness . . .

When I awoke me and Kelly were chained to the walls.
'Help,' mouthed Kelly. The monster was sharpening a sword.

The monster's face was a mouldy green, he turned it towards me. 'Hello Miss Lynzy and Miss Kelly, my name is Greeny and that is the last thing you'll ever know. Goodbye girls!'
I gulped, Kelly just stared.

Greeny's eyes began to swirl. 'You will do as I command!'
Kelly grabbed Greeny's keys and jumped on him.
'You'll pay for that!' Greeny thundered . . .

Jamie-Leigh Clarke (11)
Humberstone Junior School

THE OLD MANSION

Rowena and Sam had caught the wrong bus to a weird town. They thought it was good though because they knew where to trick or treat at Hallowe'en, which was one day away. They got off and saw a massive mansion at the end of the street. They went to a woman who looked scruffy and cold and said, 'Who lives in that mansion?'
The woman said, 'Don't go in. *Don't go in!'* in a voice getting louder, almost shouting. They quickly walked away from her thinking she was crazy.

As they were walking towards the house, people didn't stop staring.

They got there and knocked on the big wooden door. The door creaked. Something said, 'Come in children.'
They went into the big house and the door slammed behind them. They looked around with very curious, but sacred looks on their faces.

The stairs creaked. they looked up and saw a beautiful woman with black make-up and a beautiful, long dress. She said in a dark, deep American accent, 'Hi, whilst you're here will you come to my room?'

Suddenly a brick came through the window behind them, a woman said, 'Don't go up!' but by the time they looked back, the scene had changed and they were in a room with fire and they were chained to the wall!

Cliffhanger!

Imogen Clarke (10)
Humberstone Junior School

THE NIGHT OF THE LIVING ZOMBIE

Melissa had got to the two star hotel. She slumped onto the bed and yawned. Whether she slept is a mystery. Melissa opened her eyes and saw a bodiless head. She screamed! Melissa ran around the hotel into every room. Everyone had gone. Suddenly she heard a spine-chilling voice of icy coldness.

'Kill! Let me rip, scare you!'

Melissa ran, the voice forever getting louder. She tripped and scrambled for the phone. 'Police, now!' Suddenly the voice stopped, but breathing was heard instead. Melissa whispered down the phone, 'Please, there's something here.' Melissa knelt against the wall, terrified.

Suddenly an arm pushed out of the wall and tried to strangle her.

The door slammed open and the police came pouring in. One of them grabbed a knife and cut the arm. Melissa fell to the floor crying. The police pulled the stumped arm out of the wall and out slithered a moth-eaten zombie.

'Quick! Get it to the graveyard,' said the woman.

After an hour the zombie was in the ground.

Melissa's mum ran up to Melissa. 'I'm sorry I left you!' Tears ran down her cheeks. 'Let's go home.'

As soon as Melissa's head hit the pillow she fell asleep.

Suddenly she woke up. She was in her own bed! Was it a dream or not?

Isobel Walters (11)
Humberstone Junior School

A DAY IN THE LIFE OF A DOG

Imagine you're a dog. You wake up at whatever time you want, unless your master comes in. You have a stretch, yawn and then sit obediently enduring the boring times while your master is eating a melon and there is no hope of any scraps. Then the day really begins. The toaster goes on, the toast pops out and you wait for the crusts to come.

After this exciting spell you get back in bed and wait while your master cleans his teeth. When your master comes back down from the upper floor (no dog knows what is on the upper floor) you jump up and wag your tail, then you go and run in the garden when your master lets you out.

Then we reach a splitting point in the day. If it is a weekday your master will go to work at about 10 o'clock and will come back at about 4 o'clock. During this time you will play in the garden, but if it is a weekend you will watch your master gardening and occasionally he will play with you.

After all this at about two-thirty (or four-thirty if it is a weekday) you will jump into the back of a car and enjoy the highlight of a dog's day. The walk. There are so many sounds and smells. After this daily exercise you go home in the car, hope for some scraps at tea, then go to bed at whatever time you want.

Christian Preece (11)
Moor Park School

LIGHTS OUT

'Pass the spider-spread rolls, Sprutslip!' squealed Miss Pixiedo.
'Not likely, not less you pass the toad-crouching-in-the-hole-stuff.'
'Uh, get it yourself. I don't fancy getting a frog in my throat, thanks!' screamed Pixiedo rudely as the toad hopped up.
'Toad, I'm a toad,' it croaked.

The toad was putting up a good fight against being supper. Sprutslip dragged over the bowl of toad-crouching-in-the-hole-stuff and grabbed a straw off the table. He carefully prized open the toad's mouth and inserted the straw and began to blow until the toad was totally inflated. He then stuffed a cork into the toad's mouth so the air couldn't escape. Now the toad filled up the hole and couldn't squeeze out of it.

At that moment the glow worms and fireflies flickered out and the pixie burrow was pitch-dark.

Then all of a sudden a cork flew into Sprutslip's forehead and knocked him over. Then a slimy creature whizzed straight into Pixiedo's mouth. Yes, the toad had had his cork released and had been sent spinning in the air. You know how you can blow up a balloon and then let go before it's been tied, it becomes completely out of control, well it was like that!
Then light flickered back and the festivities continued.

Harriet Cannell (11)
Moor Park School

THE DAY OF THE MATCH

I walked onto the pitch, my heart was thumping. The rest of my team walked out of the changing rooms. The whole Arsenal team walked out to face us. Arsenal were in gold. We were in our home kit, red and white.

The ball was placed on the spot and the whistle blew. The match had started and Arsenal had possession. Arsenal were attacking with three people in the box. The cross came in. It was a high cross which swayed in the wind, but that was no trouble for our keeper who came off his line to punch the ball clear.

The ball came to me. I ran up the left hand side of the pitch and passed the ball to our striker Scholes. Scholes was clear from the last defender. He ran, with blistering pace, and struck the ball hard and low and it ricocheted off to an Arsenal player who kicked the ball to safety.

We took the throw in and started kicking the ball about and keeping possession, just to tease the opposition. We finally passed the ball out of defence. The ball came to Keane our midfielder. Keane ran up towards the goal and he was 30 yards out when, suddenly, one of the opposing players came flying in with his feet to tackle, but he missed the ball and caught Keane on the back of his legs, right on the stroke of half-time.

John Price (11)
Moor Park School

A DAY IN THE LIFE OF A DOG

My dog Ceri was walking down the field when she smelt something very funny. It was a rabbit. She chased it at top speed down the field. It got through the fence and sprinted onto the road. 'Wait Ceri.' *Blam!* She hit the fence at top speed. She yelped and yelped until Mum came down pulled her head out of the fence.

Now time for lunch. Ceri sits at the window. She wants to get food. She sneaks past Dad's guard and takes some ham. Dad sees her.

He throws her out and shouts, '*Bad mutt!*'

She's a big German shepherd, Ceri is. Then she sees David. She begs him to throw her ball and he does. She sprints after it six or seven times and now she's out of breath. She goes for a drink then plays footie with David and then rugby. Both times I win. Ceri has another drink and plays with Ankie.

It's nearly time for supper. She gets in the shed and waits. Then when David gets there she runs out and gets her dinner. She eats it quickly and that is when she goes to the door and barks and barks. She wants to go in. She gets in and goes to sleep.

David Thomas (11)
Moor Park School

PAUL THE TALL

Paul was five foot six. He was 11 years old and the tallest in the year (believe it or not!) He was always being teased because he was tall everyone expected him to be brilliant at sport, but Paul couldn't hit or kick a ball for his life! His best friend was Sam. He was the shortest in the year!

Sam was the best at sport, but Paul wasn't jealous because he knew Sam worked hard at his sport and trained with professionals, so he was bound to be good.
'Sam, I think we've got games next, can you please help me!'
Someone then called out, 'I will!' They must have been eavesdropping on Sam and I. *Crack!*

'Where am I? Why does my leg hurt?'
It turned out that the boy who had been eavesdropping had been the second tallest and had broken his leg. His name was George.

'Paul are you awake?' Sister Matilda was leaning over him, 'Ah, yes well the wheelchair is for you, oh I am sorry. You'll never be five foot six again!'
Paul felt tears come to his eyes. He quickly turned away.
'Don't worry about it, you'll be fine.'

'Paul, wake up!' Sam was pouring ice-cold water over his face and shouting down his ears!
'What, what Sam, I can't ever walk, or move on my own ever again!'

Emily Smith (11)
Moor Park School

A DAY IN THE LIFE OF A BUZZARD

As the first grey light of dawn falls on the valley I live in, I wake up and then preen my feathers. I see my hen and fledglings sitting across the nest from me. My hens send me out to catch some mice or the odd rabbit that strays into the small, wooded coppice in which we live. I stretch my talons and flutter my feathers to wake myself up. Then I climb out of the nest and onto the thick oaken branches of the tree my family and I live in.

Below me is a rabbit. *Breakfast* immediately flashes into my mind. The rabbit looks up as if it had heard me, but it is only a couple of crows fighting. I drop noiselessly down. I put out my talons to their full extent. I strike and the rabbit stops scrabbling instantly.

As I fly through the canopy of leafy branches and twigs on the hill nearby I see a large yellow clanking thing which belches out acrid black smoke. I know this is very bad. As I approach this thing I think this could be a predator even greater than me. I hover over it for a few seconds. Then a couple of animals climb out of it. They are carrying large buzzing objects. They walk over to my tree and stick the buzzing objects into it. I immediately fly out of my nest. My family's home has been destroyed.

Thomas Maitland (10)
Moor Park School

MENTAL OR GIFTED?

For two years now, I've been psychic, well I've been having visions.

All my friends are fine with the fact, and actually some of them think it's really helpful, for instance I can warn them if something unfortunate is going to happen.

That's not the point though, today I was at home with our repulsive babysitter Mary-Anne. When I had a vision that she was going to cut off her thumb. So I did what any decent person would have done and I told her. I really wish I hadn't known, because she went ballistic and once it had happened, that was the final straw, she phoned a mental clinic and asked for someone to collect me.

I can't believe this is happening. I'm being taken away, with no objection since my father's on a trip. Help!

I hate this place. It wreaks of disinfectant. I don't get treated like an eleven-year-old should. I get treated like a baby, kept away from everyone outside like a disease.

It's not doing anything for my self-esteem. What is it about psychics that is so alarming? Do we stand out as freaks?

Well whatever it is, I'm going to stop it by telling the world that just because we're different it doesn't mean that we're freaks or mental. We are an elite few of this race that have a rare gift, but it's their decision, their choice! I just wish for a world where everyone is accepted.

Georgina Aarvold (11)
Moor Park School

MOVING HOUSE

One morning there was an eight-year-old boy called Bobby. He was really not looking forward to moving because he had a perfect house, but they were only renting it, so they had to find a house in one week, which is pretty hard.

They found a house but they would have to do a bit of work to it, because it was in a bit of a state when they bought it. But the main thing was, it was cheap. They had all their things in the van to take to their new house.

They only saw the house in the newspaper so they didn't know what it was like inside. They had a rough idea what it was like.

In a way he was excited about moving house, but then he wasn't because he would miss his old house. He didn't want to stay the night because he thought there might be ghosts in the building, which was over 500 years old. So Bobby had to sleep in his mum and dad's bedroom.

Bobby heard a noise and thought it was his mum and dad coming back from their friend's party. But it wasn't them! It was something else. Bobby didn't see his babysitter. He knew something was wrong. The babysitter was nowhere in sight. Bobby heard something. He went up the stairs . . .

His mum and dad never saw him again and that was the last time he was ever seen.

Will Burton (10)
Moor Park School

SHORT STORY

Day one

Here I am, waiting to leave on our trip. At the moment we are stuck in a hot office waiting for a taxi. It's so boring in here, that's why I'm writing this down. Most people in here are browsing but it's all in the wrong language. I wonder if we are ever going to leave!

Day two

We have just had a night at the Posada Casita. I had to sleep in a hammock. I am now drying off from an early morning swim. In a cage I saw an ocelot.

Day three

I am lying in a bed which one of the staff gave up for me. We have just had a flight in a plane in which the fuel gauge said empty!

Day four

It's me, George, drying off again but this time from swimming under Salto Angel. I have just had my picture taken while standing next to the highest waterfall in the world. I went to Angel Falls!

Day Five

Today I am coming home from this big waterfall holiday. Returning to my holiday flat is sad, but it will be great to get home, dry and sleep on a bed. Goodnight!

Thomas Arrow (10)
Moor Park School

A Short Story

One day I was down the street, when a stranger came up to me and pulled me roughly into a portal.

After a long, windy journey of ups and downs and side to sides I reached the end. At this end I appeared to be in the same alley, but when I walked out there were goblins, hairy, scary monsters, vampires and don't forget the evil witches and wizards!

My real adventure started here, you see I had made friends with a good witch. She had told me that this is where you get dumped if you break all the codes associated with magic. The witch, called Wilba, found out how to get down and there wasn't a way back without magic, so you are stuck! Wilba told me that any magical powers get vaporised.

So now Wilba and I are trying to find a way out. We've marked out the alley that you get delivered to by the porthole. Wilba knows a place we can work privately. We have got a cauldron to work in and we have also some magic powers. Now Wilba is seeing if any of the magic works. I hope it will!

Listen! 'Fire burn and cauldron bubble,' says Wilba mysteriously.
I go to have a look and there in front of me is a great big blob of . . .
'Oh my life!'

Harry Brentnall (10)
Moor Park School

GHOST STORY

One day a boy called Tom was wandering through the wood by Moor Park with his friend Ben. They had wandered not very far when they came across a gate. Above it said *Ghost Manor*. Of course Ben and Tom ran through the gate, which had suddenly opened, it closed behind them. Ben and Tom were so excited they didn't even notice the gate.

Then Ben and Tom came to a frightening halt. Some creature howled from the inside of the manor. It was so creepy Ben and Tom started to worry, but gradually they went on.

They finally got into the forgotten manor. It was more like a haunted manor because something see-through and white was coming down the stairs. They ran all the way home and they agreed to meet there at nine o'clock the next night.

It was 9pm. They met outside the gates of the haunted manor. They got in, and explored the first room. In it was a normal kitchen, they went to the next room, there inside was a trapdoor made of wood.

They went around the manor, when suddenly a ghostly, 'Boo!' broke the silence. Ben and Tom ran as fast as they could through the trapdoor. Tom tripped over and fell on Ben. They both dropped like a stone!

The strange thing is they have never been seen again . . .

Benjamin Pratt (10)
Moor Park School

MURDER MASK

'Mummy! Listen to me Mummy!'
'What is it Kara?'
'Mummy, where's Daddy?'
'Away. Is that the phone . . .?'

Mum swept away to answer the imaginary rings. I looked up at the mask on the wall that Dad had given us two weeks ago - just before he disappeared. Where was he?

Finishing my dinner hurriedly, I dashed to my room, slamming the door behind me, blocking out my mum's sobs that she thought I couldn't hear. A tear trickled down my cheek. I'd give anything to see him again . . . anything . . .

An eerie chanting rang through the house. 'Just the wind,' I told myself firmly and sank into a restless sleep.

I woke three hours later, stiff and tired. The old grandfather clock struck midnight. As I started to snooze, I froze as a familiar scream pierced the night. It was my mum's.

Fearfully I crept down the stairs, into the kitchen, grabbing a large bread knife for protection, my face pallid and hands sweating. I peered into the darkness, the mask, it wasn't there . . .

Squeezing the knife tightly, I made my way nervously out the front door. Blood was trickling off the doorstep. The body of my mother lay before me. Her murderer stood over her laughing, wearing the mask. I recognised that laugh. It was my father's!
'You said you'd give anything!' he cackled, taking a step towards me. 'Anything!'
The mask gleamed menacingly.
This time he was coming . . . coming for me. . . .

Katie Davies (11)
Newlands Community Primary School

THE HOUSE ON THE HILL

Lisa looked in the mirror gloomily, as she combed her long, black, silky hair, with her new blue comb. Picking up her bag and mobile, she raced downstairs ready to go to school.

Hours passed, as Mum waited for Lisa and her brother to come home. That moment, Lisa and Mark were just about to race upstairs, when Dad stopped them.
'Well,' Mark blurted through the silence, 'spill the beans!'
'We have to leave for the new house tomorrow.'

The birds chirped in the trees, as a bright red car pulled up at number 7, the house on the hill. Lisa clutched her teddy bear tightly, as though something was about to go wrong. Dad, who was admiring the garden from the upstairs window, was so joyful, he was in a world of his own.
I don't know why Dad is so happy, Lisa thought, *if I had to move house, this would be the last on my list.*

Inside the house it was gloomy, it was as though it was isolated. A panel from a stair was missing, where a rat nest was formed.

A week later, at midnight, an echo filled the whole house, as the cellar door swung open. A mournful crying came from inside. It sounded just like their grandma, who had died 10 years ago. They heard footsteps coming up the staircase, and the slicing of daggers . . .

Gabrijela Borovic (11)
Newlands Community Primary School

WHAT WAS THAT?

Having walked up a five metre hill, with a ten stone suitcase, Jesse's legs and arms began to feel like snapping. Jesse finally reached the top of the hill with her mum.

'Well, that was easy,' her mum laughed, carrying a tiny make-up box, some peppermints and her sunglasses. Jesse stood up with a fake giggle. Picking her suitcase up she gasped in amazement. Jesse stared. Their new house looked like a horror house. She walked slowly to the front door, shivering. The door was dusty, like nobody had been in it for years.

Opening the front door, she stepped inside. She walked up the crooked stairs. 'This is my bedroom!' Jesse echoed down the stairs, pointing to the bedroom door. Jesse turned the handle and tiptoed inside, like a mouse.

Soon after Jesse was in her nightie ready for bed. She crept into bed, and pulled the sheets up. Jesse heard a frightening noise. She saw the moon and the stars out of the window. 'What was that? Who's there? Is that you Mum?' she whispered nervously.
The floorboards creaked. Jesse clenched the sheets and pulled them up tight onto her chest.

Finally she climbed out of bed and crept downstairs. It was dark and cold. Jesse heard a loud scream. What could she do? Her mum was in bed. She looked behind her, the door slammed. Jesse heard the same noise. She ran upstairs screaming, and locked herself in her bedroom.

Lauren McVey (10)
Newlands Community Primary School

THE BAD DREAM

'Mum, help!' I screamed as I sat up in bed.

'What is the matter?'

'He took you away again!' I bellowed.

'Don't worry, it's only a dream,' Mum reassured me.

'B-but it seemed so real,' I sobbed.

I wiped my tears on my quilt. I had to go back to sleep because it was the middle of the night. If only she knew what horrors were happening when I was sleeping.

In the morning I woke early to see my mum. When I walked in, the bed was empty, all that remained was a note saying 'Dreamer Boy', I immediately knew what had happened. My dream had come true. The letter also said 'If you want to see your mum come to the place you're most afraid of tonight'.

That night, I went to sleep with a brave mind.

'I see you've made it,' came a voice.

'Listen, I'm not afraid of you,' I snapped. Suddenly a figure in the corner began to shrink, my mum came into view.

'And another thing, I hate nightmares.'

This time the figure disorientated . . . I woke. It was morning, my mum was there. I saved her.

I never had a nightmare again, but it might be because I would not sleep without a dreamcatcher from then on.

My adventure really made me a stronger person mentally and physically.

Adam Jeffs (11)
Newlands Community Primary School

THE HAUNTED HOOK

Danny and Nicole were having a romantic night together at the cinema in New York.
'That was brilliant wasn't it Danny?' asked Nicole excitedly.
'It sure was,' replied Danny.

Approaching the car, Danny had an excellent idea. 'How about we hear some jazzy music in the car?' he asked faintly.
'Sounds great!' she replied.
They both giggled slightly as they opened the Mini's red car doors. He switched on the radio. It began. Interrupted by a sudden stop on the radio, a man spoke nervously.
'Listen, listeners, there is a man dressed in black who has just broken out of the local prison tonight. This man is easily recognised because he has a hook instead of a hand. Please contact the police if you see him.'
'Did you hear that? Take me back home now!' she declared.

Danny turned the key to start the car up. Minutes later, Danny pulled up to the kerb outside of Nicole's flat and stopped the car. 'We're home!' he shouted. No reply.

He stepped out of the car and noticed that Nicole was not in the back seat. Danny walked slowly to the car door to open it, and to his shock he came across a hook that was gripped onto the handle, glistening in the moonlight.

Danny fell back onto the wet grass. 'Arrgh!' came a cry from behind. He quickly got up from the ground and looked around him.

'Nicole, is that you?' Danny cried loudly.
Silence.

Grace Humphrey (11)
Newlands Community Primary School

THE STONE OF THE SWORDSTALKER

'So, Daniel, tell me again. Why do we have to clamber through this pyramid, then climb over a bottomless cavern with this very thin rope?' moaned John.

'We have to get the Stone of the Swordstalker. It's an ancient artefact and Professor Jones wants to put it on show at the British Museum.'

Daniel and John progressed over the cavern on top of a small cliff face. There it was, the Stone of the Swordstalker. Daniel took out a bottle of acid and poured it over the metal case that the stone was imprisoned in. The case melted away, the stone shook vigorously and exploded!

Smoke blocked their view. All they could see were two blood-red eyes. A low-pitched voice echoed around the cavern. 'I am free! The whole world will bow down to me once again!'

It stepped out of the smoke. It was at least two metres tall, purple with burgundy wings and was carrying a golden sword.

'I think this is the bit in the story where we run,' John whispered in Daniel's ear.

They scurried onto the rope and ran through a narrow passageway with the creature close behind.

'What is that thing?' John shouted.

'It's the Swordstalker!' Daniel replied.

The Swordstalker stopped. It chanted something. The statues around them shook, suddenly there was a blinding white light. The men were lifted twenty feet in the air and tossed to the ground. The light had gone. The Swordstalker towered over them and raised its sword . . .

Joseph Snuggs (11)
Newlands Community Primary School

THE SLIME

I was peddling fast now, it had started to rain and it was getting heavier by the second, as I made my way home from the market. Turning down a country lane, I rode through a deep puddle full of glass which, of course, I didn't know was there. Suddenly my tyres burst and I had to walk my bike for miles.

Finally I came to a mansion.

I decided to shelter from the rain. I wheeled my bike up to the porch, propped my bike against the wall, then knocked on the door but no one answered. I pushed the door and it flew open. 'Hello!' I yelled as my voice echoed around the house.

I stepped in to have a look around. In the living room there was an empty fire grate. I crept out to the back garden where I saw a shed. I crept in hoping to find some firewood. I found some straw and logs. I went back into the house to make a fire.

When the fire was ablaze I noticed a slime trail leading from the patio doors to the settee. Then another slime trail came through the door, but it was racing towards me. I tripped over my bag and hit my head on the floor. I sat up. It was still coming towards me. I ran, as fast as I could and never looked back.

Niall Marshalsey (10)
Newlands Community Primary School

FLOWER POWER

Lucy Scoter was a flower freak. She would rather water a plant than go ice skating. She was a boring girl. If she got a chance to get her hands mucky, she would do it.

One morning, in the summer holidays, Lucy got up early to see if her sunflower had grown overnight. As she made her way down the garden path, she saw the sunflower yawn. She stood in astonishment. She rubbed her eyes, but then the sunflower's leaves started moving up and down. She slowly walked nearer and the sunflower suddenly spoke.
'Are you looking at me?' it blurted out.
'No,' she replied.
'Why do you look so shocked then?' asked the sunflower.
'Because you're speaking,' stammered Lucy.
'So, you humans speak don't you?' she said.
'Yeah, I suppose we do.'
So she sat down, still in shock and began to have a conversation with a sunflower.

That night Lucy told her mum, but of course, her mum and her dad didn't believe her.

Next morning Lucy ran down the garden path to find Sally Sunflower dancing.
'Why are you dancing like that?' asked Lucy.
'I'm nervous,' Sally replied.
'Why?' asked Lucy?
'Well I might as well tell you. I want you to become my best friend,' she said.
'Of course I will,' cried Lucy, throwing her arms gently around Sally.

So from that day on Sally Sunflower and Lucy Scoter became secret best friends.

Grace Henson (10)
Newlands Community Primary School

THE MIDNIGHT SCARE!

Without a sound she locked all of the doors and windows, constantly watching the mysterious, dark figure walking down the path towards the house.

She woke up an hour later and could hear a rattling sound. She got up to see what it was, the window was wide open, someone may have got in, but it was very doubtful indeed. She thought it was just the wind, but then she heard a long, high-pitched creak. When she went to see what it was she caught a glimpse of a black-cloaked person at the bottom of the stairs as it slithered around the corner.

She ran back to bed and dived under the covers, gripping the bedclothes tightly. Then she heard a loud sound downstairs and, getting out of bed cautiously not to make a single sound, she crept down the stairs and snuck into the kitchen where she saw the same mysterious, dark, gloomy figure once again.

The thing viciously pounced towards her, screeching like a wild animal ready to attack. She quickly dived out of the way so as not to get killed by the vicious creature.

She ran out of the house screaming and into a farmhouse about one hundred yards down the road. The guy that lived there asked her what had happened and she explained that there was a fierce monster trying to kill her. The man suddenly dropped dead in front of her and behind him was the thing. What would she do now? She was doomed.

Ashley Webb (10)
Newlands Community Primary School

THE SECRET ATTIC

He looked at the lock on the trapdoor; he withdrew the key from his pocket and put it in the lock. It fitted.

Slowly climbing the rusty ladder he peered around the attic. He suddenly stopped to look at the figure as it came nearer and nearer.

He started to back off down the rusty ladder. When he climbed down the ladder the figure followed him. As he moved back from the ladder he stared at the figure climbing down the ladder. As the figure touched the floor he saw his face. The figure pulled out a gun from his back pocket and loaded it. Then he pulled the trigger.

His mum raced up the stairs and saw the figure walk out of the window.

Liam Hawkins (11)
Newlands Community Primary School

THE SECRET BOX

It was the lock of the box, which had been closed for over fifty years. She carefully put her hand into her coat pocket and pulled out a rusty key, and realised that it fitted the keyhole. Then she put the key into the old, dirty lock and struggled to turn it, but she did eventually.

She took a long, deep breath and looked behind her. It was clear. She opened the box and to her surprise she found a shimmering ruby with two stars next to it, but nothing else. She decided that she was going to keep the box with the ruby in it, but then she said to herself, 'No, I can't keep the box just in case it is someone's at the house up the road.'

So she left it there. Mary just could not believe that she had found a very lovely box with a shimmering ruby inside. She really, really wanted to keep it so badly. But what if it was someone's from the house and someone threw the box away? Surely no one would throw away a box like that with a ruby inside it? Finally she put it in a secret place and left it there for the next day.

Krishanne Farmer (11)
Newlands Community Primary School

THE DEAD HOTEL

'Are you coming to take the dog for a walk?' grumbled Toni. 'Looks like you're staying for today. Steven, tonight do you want to go to the dead hotel?' whispered Toni.
'The . . . dead hotel, yeah OK then, 8 o'clock?'

7 o'clock came, 8 o'clock came. Mum and Dad were asleep. Toni and Steven snuck out of the back door and walked down the road. They reached the hotel.
'Toni shall we go into the hotel?'
'Yeah come on!' whispered Toni.

They opened the dark brown, rusty, tall door. Inside was a long, dusty spiral staircase. Toni and Steven started to shake. They both walked down a narrow corridor. Walking into a messy, cobwebbed room, Toni kept on looking behind him to see if anyone was there. They turned into a large dining room.
'Can we go now?' whimpered Steven.
'Shut up you wuss!' groaned Toni.

They heard a tin roll around the kitchen. *'Arrgghhh! Run quick!'* they both screamed.
Steven tripped over a glass vase. Everything was rolling. 'Help me up, quick!' shouted Steven.
Toni helped him up. They ran to the rusty, brown, tall door. But it had locked itself. Toni got a vase and threw it at a small window. They ran for their lives.

The next morning, as Toni and Steven walked to school, they passed the spooky, dead hotel. Everything was back to normal. So Toni and Steven will never know the mystery of the Dead Hotel!

Jordane Joannides (11)
Newlands Community Primary School

TOTALLY CLEAR

I am totally clear. I'm so creepy. All my friends laugh at me, I'm so weird. It all happened when Peter Smith found a new bug that had never been discovered before. He is such a brain box. I was so jealous. So that night I snuck into school and crept into the science room to steal the bug. It had weird markings on its back.

When I got home I took the bug out of the jar. 'Ow!' I yelled. 'Blooming bug,' I muttered under my breath.

In the morning I looked into the mirror and to my horror, I was clear all over. I couldn't go to school looking like this, so I headed to the mountains with some supplies.

When I found a place to stay I explored my surroundings, but when I got back there was this stupid mutt lying on the floor. I kicked him, but he stayed there panting, trying to look cute.

A few years had passed. I trained the dog to hunt down prey and then to my amazement the dog was clear as well, but then I wasn't clear anymore. To my joy I could see my skin again, but the disease was spreading, so I could not touch the dog.

I travelled back to the town, I was so happy that the mutt came with me. As I arrived into school, everyone started to run away and they were all clear. I am so creepy.

Rebecca Hayes (11)
Newlands Community Primary School

THE HORROR OF THE MAN-EATER BUG

'Craig, have you been telling your brother about the man-eater bug again?' Faye yelled up the stairs.

'He wanted to know,' Craig replied.

Telling David off for listening was better than being told off, thought Craig. Charming the girls was a good plan so that he could scare them.

'Dinner,' Mum shouted.

'Mmm, chips, my favourite,' Craig whispered to himself.

Craig was watching TV until about seven o'clock. Then his mum shouted him to come upstairs. Craig and David put their pyjamas on.

'Should we go downstairs tonight and look for man-eater bug?' David suggested.

'No!' Craig boomed.

That night Craig heard a window smash. He ran to his mother's room, opened the door and woke his mum up.

'Mum, I'm scared. There's someone downstairs,' Craig screamed.

'Don't worry,' Faye cried.

Faye went downstairs but she didn't come back up. Craig had waited long enough; he had waited for half an hour. Suddenly he heard a noise, and then he heard his mum scream. Craig ran downstairs and came to a sudden halt. He saw this bug creature, about five feet tall. It glared at him for about forty seconds. Craig stared at his mum's body in horror; he never knew the story was real. Running as fast as he could, he felt his heart bang.

Morning had struck. They were dead in this very house. Their graves are in the graveyard still today.

Carr Craddock (11)
Newlands Community Primary School

The Secret Attic

It was the attic door that had not been opened for one hundred years.

'Dad, where is the attic in this house?' asked Martin.

'I don't know!' yelled Dad.

Suddenly, Martin looked up and saw a little black button sticking out of thick armour of paint. He pressed the button and the paint came down shattering on the floor. Some old wooden ladders dropped down, but there was a door in the way. Suddenly, Martin remembered that he saw a black, rusty key in his wardrobe when he was looking for somewhere to put his toys.

Martin climbed up the ladder with excitement and put the key in the lock. It fitted perfectly. Martin turned the key and the door creaked open. He checked that nobody was coming and crept in.

'Hey Dad, I've found the attic,' bellowed Martin.

'Great, we finally have somewhere to put our camp bed,' replied Dad.

Dad saw a glimpse of something. It was fishbones, leading to a skeleton.

'Son, I don't want to alarm you, but there is a skeleton in here,' Dad told Martin.

'I don't like this house,' whimpered Martin.

Two hours passed. Darkness fell. Martin was back into the attic. He heard footsteps coming towards him . . .

A burglar locked Martin and his parents in the attic. They were never seen again.

Alastair Wallace (11)
Newlands Community Primary School

THE FORBIDDEN CHAMBERS OF THE UNDERGROUND

I was cold, I was scared but I could not stop. It was like someone or something was pushing me. The hairs on my arms were standing up on end and an icy shiver ran down my spine. But still this didn't stop me. I just had to see what was at the end of this narrow passage . . .

There it was - a large wooden door with a dusty, worn brass knocker and a sign saying *Knock if you dare!*

I went to knock but the door slowly creaked open. I slowly stepped through the opening. It slammed shut behind me. I couldn't see a thing. I began to scramble along the floor, but I was trapped.

A beam of light emerged from the darkness. Was I looking at ghosts coming from the pitch-black?
The ghost nervously said, 'I've been wandering these corridors for what seems forever.'

I stood up, it was still there. I pinched myself. It wasn't a dream. But how could I possibly be able to see a ghost?
The ghost gasped, 'You'd better know how. Take a look into a mirror which I clenched in the palm of my hand.'

I found I could see the wall behind me. I had no reflection!

Graham Dowers (11)
Newlands Community Primary School

DEAD ENDING

'Mum, I'm going down to Sam's house to play,' shouted Matt as he slammed the door behind him.

'Matt, Matt!' yelled Mum angrily. She didn't know what to do with him. He was meant to wash the plates and dishes. He was always going down to Sam's. They had been friends for ages. Before she could tell him he couldn't go round, he had already gone.

Matt was barging down the road, knocking down everyone he saw. He finally reached Sam's house and had no one else to knock over.

Sam heard loud bangs at the door. He knew it was Matt by the way he knocked. You'd know if you were Sam. They were very alike and liked the same things. They did everything together. Matt and Sam were always down the park. Matt had slept round Sam's more times than he had slept at his own house.

Now they headed down to the park again to play football. Sam kicked the ball so hard that it went into somebody's garden. *Bang!*
'You go!' screamed Sam.
'You kicked it!' shouted Matt.
'It's your ball,' wailed Sam.
They finally decided to both go.

Matt and Sam were going to knock but the door suddenly opened. They slowly walked in. They stepped into a red circle. *Crash!* Something very heavy landed on them.

When they woke up they climbed to their feet and were staring at their bloody bodies. They realised the awful truth. They were no longer alive!

Ben Spicer (11)
Newlands Community Primary School

THE UNREVEALED THINGS

He looked at the ancient lock on the darkened door and thought the key fitted in the hole. He withdrew the key and placed it in the lock. It fitted. He turned with two hands because it was hard to turn. It opened. Anxiously he opened the door and a veil of cobwebs obscured his view. Brushing them to one side, he peered into the darkness.

At first he did not see anything so he looked again. There was something and it looked horrifying. It had a square shape and it was very old, very rusty and clear to see. As he approached the object he was wondering if anything would happen like a surprise. He pushed the cobwebs to one side and there was a box . . . a treasure box. There was a keyhole with the key on top. He placed the rusty key inside the keyhole and turned the key.

As he opened the box it was full of gold, lots of gold. He grabbed handfuls and shoved them in his pocket. When the box was nearly empty he saw a tail. He touched it. It hissed back. It was a giant, twenty-five foot snake, the most venomous snake in the world ready to kill him because the secret had been revealed - the secret that no one knows, and nobody should know.

He was never seen again.

Ashley Warren (10)
Newlands Community Primary School

THE WOODS

Dad burst through the door, dropping his briefcase in the doorway.
'What a wonderful day!'
Clare was surprised to see her dad so happy. She ran after him up the stairs.
'What is going on?' Clare demanded.
Dad turned and looked at her. 'I've invited your stepmother to stay.'
She was about to knock herself out when the stepmother arrived. Clare was pretending to be asleep, but instead she was preparing to run away.

At midnight she slyly crept out of the house and ran to the woods.

Soon after, she was standing in a dull, dark, haunted place. She stood shaking like a leaf in the wind. *Crack!* 'What was that?' She shivered as she looked into the distance. There stood a black figure. 'Oh help!'

Clare's heart beat faster and faster. A cold, wet tear tricked down her face. She stumbled over a branch. Slowly she opened her eyes - the black figure hovered over her. *Oh I wish I was at home now*, Clare thought to herself, as she panted heavier each time she thought about what was going to happen to her. Clare jumped to her feet. But it didn't matter how fast she ran, the black figure stayed right behind her. Clare archly peeped over her shoulder again, running as quickly as her feet would take her. The figure leapt towards her.
'Help!'

Danielle Starkey (11)
Newlands Community Primary School

THE NIGHTMARE HOUSE

'Keep up!' shouted Jon to his little sister, Poppy. As she ran to keep up something caught Jon's eye. It was a banner hung up on the hedge saying *Michael's Magnificent Fairground, Friday and Saturday.* Jon beamed then grabbed Poppy's hand and made a dash for their house.

'Dad?' he called opening the door. 'Can we go to the fair this Saturday?'

'As long as your homework's done,' Dad said.

It was a long wait till Saturday.

'Hurry up,' said Jon impatiently, as he waited for Poppy to find her shoes.

When they arrived Dad gave them both money. They looked around wondering which ride to go on first, when horror music came to their ears. Jon ran up to the man taking the money and soon they were in 'The Nightmare House' riding on a cart.

It was the darkest place they had ever been in, there was the faint smell of garlic. It was the chill that got to them. There were echoes and strange noises they had never heard before. Suddenly the lights went out, the cart stopped and there was complete silence. It was scarier than the spooky noises. Then from the darkness came the glimmer of a lantern. Nearer and nearer it came, and . . . a hooded figure. It spoke, 'Stay there.' It lowered its hood and took off its fluorescent scull mask, Jon and Poppy screamed.

'It's only me, I knew you would be here,' said their dad with a grin!

Annie White (10)
Newlands Community Primary School

THE TROUBLE TWINS, THE GHOST TWINS

'It's not much,' said Anne looking around the cold, damp old house while turning the rugged fire on.

'Damn it!' Jane shouted, she had banged her long legs on the coffee table; her hair came up to her legs and was brown. Her sister Anne had brown eyes and hair and was wearing a green dress, Jane was wearing a yellow dress.

'Huh, I hate this place,' Anne said wafting a newspaper round.

Suddenly twin ghosts came down, they both had black hair and green eyes, one with a pink dress, one with a black dress. Jane was hugging Anne with fear.

'Oh dear!' screamed Anne.

'Who are you?' whispered Jane.

'Nei Nei and Ne Na,' whispered the one with pink on.

That night Anne had a nightmare that she was going to get killed by those ghostly things. She opened her eyes; in reality there was one of the ghosts above her. She could not scream, and then something stabbed her. She was dead now, not even a cold-hearted ghost.

Nei Nei laughed, 'The Trouble Twins strike again!'

Nei Nei and Ne Na shivered, the main ghost was coming, Lilly. There was a flash of thunder and there she was. She had blonde hair and a white dress. 'You never come here again!' she shouted. Nei Nei and Ne Na disappeared.

The fire started, Anne was alive.

Holly Ball (9)
Newlands Community Primary School

FAIRY SWORD

3000 years ago.

The bloody sword fell clanging on the rocky ground. The fairy heart pierced with blood, she tumbled and then *puff!* The fairy had disappeared.

Year 2003

Charlie was excited, the new well had been built, and he was going to watch the opening.

The mayor stood in his new blue suit, his chains around his neck glittering in the sun. He cut the ribbon and Charlie stared, something was down there. He clambered over the wall and down, down, down he went. He missed the mini sword and kept on falling. *Thud!* Charlie had landed on something soft.

'Ow,' said a hoarse voice, 'get off me.'
Charlie was pushed onto the damp gravel.
'Get me out of here,' Charlie yelled at a little purple man in a yellow coat and a pair of pink gloves.
'Ask the leader to give you the sacred sword, that will take you back to the surface, but you have to keep it with you at all times, the fairy queen didn't and it stabbed her!'
Charlie rushed down the tunnel and asked the leader to give it to him.

In a flash Charlie vanished, in a few seconds he was zooming through a cylinder of colours, red, blue, yellow and green. Now he was back at the top with his mum and dad.

'Come on,' cried his mum.
'Hang on!' Charlie said as he shoved the mini sword in his pocket and from then on he always kept it with him!

Elizabeth Mousley (10)
Newlands Community Primary School

THE DEVIL

Knock knock knock. 'Hello, who's there?'
'It's Hannah, so let me in.'
Anne opened the door and Hannah ran upstairs to her room.
'How was school?' Anne shouted up the stairs.
'Fine,' she replied.

At teatime Hannah didn't come downstairs for tea. Anne thought it was a bit strange, but didn't think anything of it. When Anne went to go to bed she heard some poles clatter in the basement. She opened the basement door and turned on the light and peered down the steps, but she couldn't see anything.

Next day Anne came downstairs and noticed the same noise she had heard the day before. She tried to open the basement door but it wouldn't budge. Then, all of a sudden, the door swung open and she tripped down the stairs and bashed her head on the wall, which knocked her unconscious.

After half an hour she woke up to see a glowing pair of bright yellow eyes. The black evil devil wrapped his long fingers round her neck and dragged her up the basement steps. Then *smash!* He threw her out of the bedroom window; then he crumbled up into a pile of ash on the floor and was carried off in the wind.

The mangled body of Anne remains lying in a pool of blood in the backyard.

Adam Saunt (10)
Newlands Community Primary School

THE KNIGHT OF MAIDENSVILLE

Once upon a time in an old, dilapidated house there lived a boy called Embro, a slave. One day a letter arrived, it said -

'Dear Embro

You have a new master. He is . . . the Duke of Maidensville, he will arrive tomorrow.

From the King of Maidensville'

The next day he arrived, like the letter had said. For the first time ever he had to go to Semons Castle because slaves weren't allowed to go to huge castles in the world. He was so excited he couldn't wait.

When he arrived the Duke said, 'Our quest is to kill the North Ogre.'
'Erm . . . OK,' said Embro.

The next day he was given a dagger and a wooden shield, they set off. They followed the road for miles, when they finally arrived at the North Ogre's cave.

Embro had to go in first to make sure that the cave was safe.
'All clear,' Embro shouted as it echoed to the Duke.
'OK we will camp here and set the trap in the morning,' said the Duke.

The next morning they set the net up for Ogre. When the Ogre came he fell into the trap and Embro chopped the Ogre's head off. They took the head back to prove that Embro was worthy of being a knight.

The king said, 'I knight you Embro the Duke of Maidensville,' and he went on to marry the daughter of the king and became a prince, and they lived happily ever after.

Jack Dorman (10)
Newlands Community Primary School

THE WISH OF DOOM

'Four eyes, four eyes,' the children cheered madly at an 11-year-old boy called John, at Plumpton Junior School.

'Leave, me, alone,' he shouted, as the children burst out laughing. He ran off towards an old oak tree, where he slid down behind it and started crying. He fished in his pocket for a tissue, but instead he found a moonstone that his grandma gave him before she died.

Clutching it tightly, he made a wish. As he carefully wrapped the moonstone in his tissue, he heaved himself to his feet and noticed that his body was fading away! He cried out for help, but not a soul came. His feet started to fade away first! Then his legs, arms, hands and head! Pulling the moonstone out of his jeans pocket, once more, it started to form bright blood-red smoke inside.

It swirled and swirled, like a witches' cauldron. It bubbled and bubbled, until it let off a puff of thick, red smoke. He started to fade away faster and flicker like a badly connected TV. He only had his eyes left, and swung round to the opposite side of the tree. The playground was deserted.

In the next second, he was gone. He had disappeared into thin air. All that was left was the moonstone, lying on the ground, with a small face of a boy peering out. He looked as if he was terrified. White pale face and wide eyes.

Ariane Holder (11)
Newlands Community Primary School

THE NEW HOUSE

It was the day that Sarah and her family were moving into the new house. It was on the hills in Wales. Sarah was not looking forward to moving, she had heard some funny things about the house. As they were driving up to the cottage it was dark, dull and raining.

Sarah had to sleep on the floor that night, because they didn't have any beds, everything was still in the van. She couldn't get to sleep that night. After about an hour of tossing and turning she got up to get a drink from the bathroom. The floors were creaking as she walked along the wooden landing, step by step.

Suddenly she heard a noise, she jumped and turned around and she saw a sudden movement. Sarah followed in its direction; it was heading for the spare room. Sarah moved softly and silently towards the spare room. She followed what appeared to be an old lady ghost. The ghost opened the wardrobe door, but it wasn't really a wardrobe door, it led down to some sort of dungeon.

Sarah crept down the steps, down to the darkness beneath. The ghost whispered to Sarah. She moved closer and closer. The ghost backed off. She felt a hand on her shoulder and gasped.
'Sarah, breakfast,' called Mum from behind her.

At the breakfast table Sarah was thinking about the ghost. 'What could it have been?'
'What did you say love?'
'Nothing Mum, just thinking.'

Brittany Green (10)
Newlands Community Primary School

THE GHOSTLY SHADOWS

'Mum, Mum,' Adam ran like a rocket.
'What, what?' Mum shouted.
'I am in the football team this year.'
'Oh well, we're sorry Son, you can't be.'
'Why not?' asked Adam.
'Because tomorrow we are moving, sorry Son.'
'But, but . . .' sighed Adam, as he ran up the stairs.

A few seconds later Dad walked through the door.
'Where's Adam?' Dad happily said taking his coat off.
'We need to start packing for tomorrow,' answered Mum.

The next day, at the new house, at round about teatime, Dad asked Adam whether he liked his room.
'Yes,' Adam replied, 'I can have a computer now I have a bigger room. If I have a computer then I can keep in touch with my mates.'

That night he saw dark and mysterious shadows lurking over him, he closed his eyes tightly shut thinking it was a dream. Opening his eyes slowly and cautiously he glimpsed the shadow still hovering before him. He tried to go to sleep but it didn't work. He got up and ran to his mum crying that he wanted to go back to his old house.

Luckily the next night he didn't see the shadows again and soon the new house began to feel like home.

Chelsea Geary (10)
Newlands Community Primary School

THE HAUNTED HOUSE

One day, on Tuesday night, the sisters went to bed, then the door creaked. One of the sisters lay in bed thinking about why her mother told her to stay away from her old house. Then she woke up and looked on the floor. It was something round and red. It looked like blood, but it wasn't, it was one of her old toys. 'Thank goodness,' she said to herself.

The next day they were all downstairs watching TV and they heard the dog bark from upstairs. 'What is it Floppy? Floppy, what is it boy?'
'Woof,' the dog barked again.
'What is it Floppy?'
Then it all went quiet. Mum went upstairs to see what was the matter. It was just the trees rustling and the window slamming. They then heard a voice from outside, but only Mum and the dog heard it, it sounded like a witch.

It came and it went every day. In the night, when they were trying to sleep, they kept hearing the sounds of voices of witches. It went on every day and every night until the next day when she was really scared. In the end one of her sisters dressed up as a witch in the night. At the end of the day they all admitted that it was very scary indeed!

Karl Fletcher (10)
Newlands Community Primary School

THE BLOODY DAGGER

It was nine o'clock and time for Sam to go to bed. He walked up the stairs and cleaned his teeth. He crept into his room, trying not to wake anyone. Then to his amazement he noticed a zombie walking up and down his room, who then disappeared into thin air. Sam ran as quickly as he could downstairs and he slept on the settee, all night worrying.

The next morning, he told his mother. She said, 'Not to worry.'
He went to school not worrying about it.

Sam went home and played on his PlayStation until bedtime.

He saw the zombie for weeks and weeks until he noticed that the zombie hung in the air. A dagger behind it started chasing him around the house until he fell down the stairs and the dagger went straight through Sam's back.

The next morning, Mum noticed blood on the floor. She lifted up the sofa to reveal Sam on the floor, dead. She fell to the ground and died instantly.

Oliver Whitehead (10)
Newlands Community Primary School

WHY?

'Thirty minutes,' a voice crackled over the radio, 'you have thirty minutes left to live.' There was a long and eerie silence that fell over the hall, in which nobody, except for the tiny baby who was totally oblivious to the fact that something terrible was about to happen, moved a muscle. *This is it,* thought Megan, glancing momentarily at her baby sister. 'Oh, if only she could be spared, she is so small.'

It was all Megan's fault that this was happening now. She had made enemies with the leader of a group, who had the power to do anything they liked in their country, Hamadi. Many people despised her now, for they were about to die and everything they had worked for would be gone.

'Twenty minutes,' the voice crackled once again. Now a sense of panic set in. Screams pierced ears like foghorns sounding on a misty night.

'Ten minutes.' The sound of the man's voice echoed round the room. The screams grew louder. Nobody was quiet except for the little baby. Nobody noticed the baby anymore - they were all too busy saying final goodbyes to relatives and friends.

'One minute.' Silence. Suddenly a high cackling laugh broke the terrible silence that hung over the hall.

The bomb hit. Onlookers saw nothing. No bodies. No rubble. Just the baby. The only survivor.

Alice Grewcock (10)
Newlands Community Primary School

SAFE JOURNEY

Slowly walking out of the aircraft Aisha lifted her head to see her new home for the first time. Since her family had been killed in the horrific Bali bombing she had never truly had a proper home.

Aisha wandered around the runway where she was greeted by frantic waving from Susan, her social worker. 'How are you?' asked Susan.
'A bit shaken up, but I don't understand. Where's my new family?' replied Aisha.
'Getting their house ready for you, I suppose,' Susan told her. 'Now come on, we'd better get you to your new home. I should think you're dying to meet your foster parents.'

Driving to their next destination, thoughts of her beloved family and the horrific bombing in her beautiful country flooded her mind. However hard she tried she couldn't get rid of the visions of that dreadful night, the night her entire family had . . . She couldn't bring herself to think about it. She still had the scars from that painful event.

Two cups of cocoa and chocolate biscuits later, Aisha was starting to get to know her new family. Mr and Mrs Karhesh were very welcoming and, for once, Aisha felt safe. She felt she could be herself around them.

Mr and Mrs Karhesh had never been able to have children but they had adopted a boy called Nathan. When he was killed in a car crash two years ago they felt it was their duty to adopt Aisha. She was now safe.

Hannah Mason (11)
Newlands Community Primary School

TERROR OF THE NIGHT

She lay motionless in her bed listening to the owls screeching into the night. It's hard trying to sleep when you're petrified. She was just dozing off when the clock struck twelve. She wondered if she would ever get to sleep.

Suddenly she identified a loud clanking sound from outside. She crept up to the window, questions racing through her mind. Do I dare look beyond the curtains? Surprised by her actions she ripped back the curtains. She let out an ear-piercing scream. She was confronted with a figure, dressed in black, with white pallid lips and a clammy face. What could she do?

Slowly the figure heaved himself into the room, his eyes like a deep black hole that never ended. Terrified of what would become of her if the figure came any closer, she picked up the vase and smashed it upon the figure's head. She let out a silent scream. Petrified she faced what was to come. The figure reached for her face, she grabbed for his hand, but too late. The figure drew a dagger from his pocket, his menacing eyes growing ever wider. She knew he meant to kill her.

In the scuffle, which broke out between them, she somehow managed to grab hold of the dagger. In one last violent attempt to escape she lunged forward and stabbed the figure. He screamed as it pierced his heart. A surge of relief ran through her as she stood over the figure's body, which was now oozing out blood. The figure was dead.

Stacy Lees (11)
Newlands Community Primary School

SCARE!

On the 21st of May the President of the USA received a letter containing terrifying news. It read . . .

'Dear Mr President I shall scare a hundred women to death by the end of the year. You will have to free my mother from prison, to save others'.

The President looked shocked - there weren't any women in prison at the minute. The letter wasn't signed.

'I don't like it Lisa.' Andrea shivered, as she walked down Diamond Alley. 'Haven't you heard, in the newspapers a man is going to scare a hundred people to death?' She stood dismayed as her sister gave her a pathetic look.
'Don't be so stupid!' Lisa sighed. Her paranoid sister was started to irritate. 'It's just a dumb rumour, that's all.'

Cautiously moving towards the end of the alleyway, Lisa felt that something wasn't right. A distant howl pierced the darkness like a sharp knife through butter.

Standing in front of them was a man, red eyes glinting towards the misty moon. A scream. It wasn't loud enough. No one could help them now. They started to run, but the man was right behind. Suddenly he pounced. For Andrea it was too late.

The body of the first of many victims lay on the ground.

It had begun . . .

Helen Ball (11)
Newlands Community Primary School

THE MIDNIGHT SUCKER

Midnight. Nothing moved. The vampire slid from under the bed. Everyone was asleep. The vampire hung over the sleeping boy. 'Hey . . . zzz . . . get off my pizza . . .' Still asleep the boy smacked his hand out of the way. Dracula knew that this would be harder than he thought. Then . . . the boy sat up, slipped out of bed, fetched a glass of water before climbing back into bed. He had just pushed his luck, Dracula poured the water over the boy.

'Yo dude! Can't you see I'm trying to sleep around here!' the boy yelled. Dracula was not used to being talked to like this.
'What's your name human?' he demanded.
'The name's Niall,' the boy answered coolly.
'Aren't you afraid?' Dracula mouthed. 'I mean I'm a vampire. I could bite you at any time.'
'Is that a threat buddy, because downstairs there's a huge bag of garlic, just waiting for you.' Niall heard the vampire's hissing.
'Don't you threaten me human, anything you can do I can do it better!' Dracula roared.
Niall sneered back, 'Really, could you find a girlfriend?' Dracula turned red with rage. 'You know the garlic is starting to sound a fab idea.' Now Dracula was a dark purple colour.

Niall walked up to the window and pulled back the curtains, 'Well, what a great way to start the morning!'
'Morning!' Dracula screamed, exploding into dust.
'That's a shame,' Niall sighed at the pile of dust, 'I was just starting to like him.'

Laura Graham (11)
Newlands Community Primary School

PIZZA MAN!

'Dad why do you have to go now? I don't want to be left on my own!'
It was 10.30 on Saturday night and Ashley's dad had been called out to
work, meaning Ashley was all alone.

Feeling peckish, Ashley decided to order a pizza. After taking about 10
minutes to decide which to have, she finally chose pepperoni and
dialled the number into the phone. It was answered straight away by a
very gruff man. 'Hello, Pizza Hut!'
'Hello, I would like to order a pepperoni pizza please,' she replied.
After giving her address she put down the phone.

Eleven o'clock, still no sign of the pizza! Finally a loud knock came
from the front door. Ashley opened the door to reveal who it was and
then went upstairs to find the money. Walking out of her bedroom she
heard an ear-piercing scream from the front door. Looking over the
banister Ashley could see a pizza cutter being brought down and then
the house was silent again.

As quick as a flash the pizza man started bounding up the stairs towards
her, the pizza cutter in his hand! Ashley didn't know where to go or
what to do. If he'd murdered one person, he was bound to murder
another!

The clock chimed midnight. Ashley's dad walked in the front door and
started to shout her. No reply. He shouted again. Still no reply! That's
when he decided to look for her.

He found her . . . dead. The pizza cutter covered in blood beside her!

Faye Warner (10)
Newlands Community Primary School

THE GREAT FLIGHT

England 1941.

Bombs were dropping, gunfire and gas attacks; they were all the things happening during the Second World War when Germany declared war over England.

Jim and his mum were moved to the countryside away from all the madness, but Jim's dad was in the middle of it all, he was a bomber and was bombing Germany and all air bases.

Jim couldn't help thinking about his dad. It was distracting him from his schoolwork - not even his mum could do that. He was a bit of a geek. He was getting tired of worrying about his dad, until it came, a letter telling them of his dad's capture in a German air base, outside of Berlin. Jim struggled to hold back the tears until finally he burst out crying. He had a plan. He put his coat on and ran out the door.

He made his way to an airfield then stole a plane and headed for Germany. At last he was flying over Germany. He took the plane down, down, down, finally crashing into the ground.

Ryan Gallagher (11)
Newlands Community Primary School

CHRISTMAS EVE

Once upon a time, in a small village, there was a brother and sister called Sally and John. They lived in quite a small house.

It was Christmas Eve, everyone was excited about the next day. Sally and John had their friends and family round, they had loads of food, like sausage rolls, chocolate cake and so on.

When everyone was gone, Sally whispered to John, 'I hope Santa got me what I wanted.'
'Me to,' replied John.
They both went to bed with a smile on their faces.

The next morning they both ran down the stairs yelling, 'He's been, he's been.'
They burst inside the living room. There the presents were, lying in a heap by the lit Christmas tree. John lunged for the first present he saw. It was a Barbie doll. 'Yuck,' he bellowed.
Sally picked one up. 'An Action Man, yuck!'
'I want that Action Man,' cried John.
'I want that Barbie Doll,' cried Sally.
'Wait,' yelled Dad.
'Listen, your presents must have got mixed up somehow, so why don't you swap your presents? Then you'll get what you wanted,' said Dad.

They sat there for hours and hours playing.

Gemma Baker (9)
Newlands Community Primary School

NINE-YEAR-OLD TROUBLE!

Monday morning Sophie woke up to hear, 'Ahhh, ohhh.' It was her mum, 'What's . . . ?'

'Go away!' shouted her mum.

Later Sophie heard her mum on the phone, 'Yes please, 2.30pm, brilliant.'

Sophie went to school in a bad mood still shouting at her mum. That made Mum's neck even worse. When Mum got back home she nearly died with pain so she went straight to the doctors.

When she got there, there were another nine mothers waiting. One of the mother's asked, 'What's the matter with you? A pain in the neck? Me too.'

Then Mum was called for her turn. She went in.

'Now what's the matter with you?' asked the doctor.

'A pain in the neck,' replied Mum.

'Have you got a daughter?'

'Yes,' replied Mum.

'Well, that is what's the matter,' explained the doctor. 'I have got just the thing for you,' the doctor said with delight. The doctor gave Mum the only known cure, a box of chocolates!

The next day all nine-year-old girls were watching television after school. Suddenly the screen turned black, a magician appeared. Now all the girls had been hypnotised by the magician's magic words, 'Zee zaa zoose, calumbra.' The magician raised his hands followed by a puff of smoke.

The next day the girls were back to their old selves. 'Let's hope that never happens again,' said Mum, with a huge sigh of relief, 'being a parent is no way an easy task!'

Amanda Stubbs (9)
Newlands Community Primary School

THE MYSTERIOUS BALL

'What a massive house,' I said. A mansion stood before my eyes. I'm Phil and over there is my stupid pathetic 10-year-old sister Jessica.
'I can't wait to get inside that house,' my stupid sister said.
'Hey,' I shouted, 'I'm going to be the first one inside the new house.' I ran to the front door and touched it.

The house was pitch-black, Jessica ran into the house and flicked on the lights.
'Whoa,' I gasped, 'this place is huge.' My mum and dad had come inside with loads of boxes in their hands.
'Well, what do you think?' asked Mum.
'Very big,' I replied.
Five hours later the moving men had put our furniture in place.

Later that night I found a ball in the corner of my new room, I studied it for a moment, it was the size of a walnut.

The next day I woke up and ran down the stairs. Suddenly I missed a step and fell head first into the window. When my mum came down the stairs she fainted. It was because of that stupid ball. I saw all this from my spirits. The ball was at the bottom of the stairs waiting to be used again.

Kevin Vickers (10)
Newlands Community Primary School

WHO?

Honey gazed out of the window at the polluted skies and skyscrapers. The summer holiday seemed so far away. She was going to stay with her cousin Mandy.

Finally the summer holiday arrived and Honey left by train for Devon. She would not miss her city life much.

Mandy was waiting for her to arrive. Two hours later Honey arrived. Looking from head to toe at Mandy, she laughed. 'We definitely need to go shopping while I'm here!'

A day later the two girls were playing on the farm when one of the horses went missing. They started to look, searching high and low. Honey asked, 'What's so great about the horse anyway?'
Mandy replied, 'It's one of Dad's prize-winning jumpers!'
'So?'
'So, we've got to find it!' she cried.

Night fell upon the garden once again and the girls were safely tucked up in bed, when Mandy was woken by a bang, crash and an ear-piercing scream.

The next day, the girls woke early and ran outside in their PJs to find the prizewinner with a pool of blood laying around him. 'Who? What could do such a thing?' sobbed Mandy, starting to cry.

Weeks passed and more blood pools lay around the farmyard. That night the girls were looking out of the bedroom window. Shadows moved on the wall behind them. They slowly turned around to find a tall man standing over them.

A piercing scream woke the family. They rushed in to find just the bodies.

But who was the murderer?

Abigail Shardlow (11)
Newlands Community Primary School

TAKEN

I live on a mountain, because up here those bloodsuckers can't get me. Of course you know who I mean by those bloodsuckers, don't you? If not I'll tell you, the vampires.

It all happened on a sunny day, just like today. Somebody found a small diamond, which they picked up and put in their pocket - a fairly normal thing to do wouldn't you say? Not today. Nobody knew, but it was a very special diamond. It had the power to unleash one hundred vampires with one rub.

On that morning Peter, the boy who has never been found since, rubbed the diamond. It is said that on that night, a vampire was seen in his room taking him somewhere. He has never been found by the police or anybody. Indeed, three policemen who set out in search of the boy, never returned, ever!

One day, an extremely brave man said that he was going to find them, even if it took his life. It's written that he actually found the place, but he slipped on a mountain peak and plummeted 1,000 feet to his death. The place is supposed to be written in his diary. Rumour has it that he took that with him. Many others have looked but none have returned and never will. That is why I'm staying here like I said before. Here they can't get me. The mystery will never be solved.

Emma Mangham (11)
Newlands Community Primary School

HOW THE BUTTERFLY GOT HIS WINGS

One day there was a caterpillar, his name was Bob the Caterpillar. He lived in a garden, because he liked eating the grass, and it was cosy and warm.

One day he went for a walk when something began growing on his sides. They looked like hearts and thin sticks with pompoms on the top. He flapped his wings and flew away.

Now he was called Bob the Butterfly.

Chamaine Geary (9)
Newlands Community Primary School

HOW THE CHEETAH GOT SO FAST

One day in the jungle cheetah was playing with the butterflies. The butterflies led him to a place where there were loads of wildebeests to eat, but on his way down he fell down a hill and landed in some magic mud.

When he got out he could run a lot faster, this meant that he could catch and eat lots of wildebeests and he was so happy.

The magic mud had a secret ingredient that made all the animals faster.

Ryan Hextall (9)
Newlands Community Primary School

HOW THE JAGUAR GOT ITS PAW PRINTS

One day a jaguar called Aaron was walking through the jungle when he saw he had no footprints, but all his family had footprints though. Then he walked home thinking.

He woke up early in the morning and saw his tiger friend, Dave. He asked, 'Want a race?'
'Bring it on,' said Dave.

'3, 2, 1! Go!'
They raced but then Aaron saw footprints behind him. It was just the wind yesterday blowing the sand over his footprints.

And Dave? He just ran off!

Luke Armstrong (9)
Newlands Community Primary School

How The Monkey Got His Tail

One day the monkey was swinging from tree to tree when his tail got stuck between two branches. He called for his friends who pulled the monkey free, but his tail got left behind.

The next day he was eating worms and one got stuck to his bottom and his tail began to grow back. This is how the monkey got his tail.

Max Dorman (8)
Newlands Community Primary School

HOW THE BABOON GOT HIS RED BUM

Once there was a baboon that had a terrible mum. The baboon sat on some jam, but he didn't know that.

He looked at his bum in the mirror and he tried to rub it off, but it wouldn't come off. It was stuck. He asked his mum to get it off, but she couldn't get it off and that is how the baboon got his red bum.

Nicky Wright (9)
Newlands Community Primary School

HOW THE TIGER GOT HIS STRIPES

The tiger was pale black and he was playing in the jungle. His name was Stripy but he didn't have any stripes so all the other tigers kept on laughing at him.

He ran into a painting when the painter was having something to eat. He had made a big hole and the painters came and painted stripes on him because he was angry.

Louis DiSalvo (8)
Newlands Community Primary School

WHY THE RABBIT HOPS

Once there was a rabbit who wanted to be fast because of all the races he went in he always came last and got laughed at.

One day he decided that if he could hop he could go faster, so he tried to hop, but all he could do was a little jump on the spot because if he jumped forward he just fell over.

If he wanted to win the race he needed to become a good hopper and a fast hopper. He practised every day for a month but he was still the world's worst hopper.

One day he went to the church before and he couldn't get up the stairs. He tried so hard that he bumped his knee and had a limp, and hopped everywhere.

That's why the rabbit hops.

Toby Snuggs (9)
Newlands Community Primary School

WHY DO LEOPARDS HAVE SPOTS?

Once upon a time there was a leopard with no spots. Leopards always laughed at him. One day he had a disease because he had spots everywhere. The monkey said, 'You've got spots!'
The leopard replied, 'I haven't.' Then he ran away into the jungle.

Every time he saw the animals he said, 'I haven't got spots!'
They all said, 'Yes you have!' But every time they said yes he got upset.
'No I haven't!' he cried one day, he wasn't going to go back to his family. He decided to hunt for himself. When he was catching something he saw himself in the river, he did have spots after all!

Mathew Ekin (9)
Newlands Community Primary School

HOW DID THE BEE GET HIS STRIPES?

One hot sunny day Bee was looking for his best friends, Ant, Ladybird and Grasshopper to play a game of ring toss. The little yellow, fluffy bee searched everywhere and finally he found them all playing underneath a rare mushroom.

'Hello,' said Bee. 'Are we still playing ring toss today?'
'Yes,' his friends replied so Bee stuck out his tail and Ant, Ladybird and Grasshopper each took turns at throwing little black rings at Bee's tail.

When they had all had enough of playing ring toss Ant tried to take the rings off Bee but they were all stuck. Ladybird and Grasshopper tried too but they couldn't get them off, so they left them on.

From that day on you could see bees with the black rings on their bodies.

Daniel Wright (9)
Newlands Community Primary School

HOW THE SUN GOT INTO THE SKY

Once there were four children called Ben, Joe, Daniel and Ash. One day they blew huge bubbles and watched the bubbles float up into the air.

They then all looked up and saw something in the sky. It was something red and fiery and fast. Then it hit all the bubbles and nearly popped them, but then it came back again and hit all the bubbles. It was a meteorite. The meteorite popped all the bubbles and they were set on fire. They formed a sun and that's how the sun got in the sky.

Benjamin Harding (9)
Newlands Community Primary School

HOW GIRAFFE GOT HIS LONG NECK

One day Giraffe was walking through the jungle when he saw a tree with green luscious leaves on it. Giraffe tried to reach for the leaves but he just couldn't reach, he was just too small. Giraffe decided to try and find another tree, so he carried on walking. On the way he met Monkey. Giraffe said Monkey, 'Do you know where there are some trees like that one but smaller?'

'Yes,' said Monkey, 'come on follow me.'

Giraffe followed Monkey until they came to another tree. Giraffe tried again but he was still too small so he tried jumping. He jumped four times. The fifth time he jumped he got his head stuck in-between two branches. He struggled to get free, but he couldn't, he was stuck.

Then Monkey came. 'Monkey,' said Giraffe, 'can you help me get out?' said Giraffe worriedly.

'I'll try but it will be tricky.'

Monkey grabbed Giraffe's legs and pulled. Every time he pulled Giraffe he got longer than before. Monkey said, 'Sorry, I am not strong enough, but I know who is.'

Monkey went to get his friends, Rhino, Hippo and Tiger and came back with them and told them to help him get Giraffe out so they did.

Monkey grabbed Giraffe's legs and Rhino grabbed Monkey. Hippo grabbed Rhino and Tiger grabbed Hippo and they pulled and pulled until *pop* his head was free from the tree. When he stood up he was as tall as a tree. That's how Giraffe got his long neck and from this day forward he's still got his long neck.

Jade Morse (9)
Newlands Community Primary School

THE MAGIC CAT

One morning Wilf and Wilma went round to Biff and Chip's house and they were playing with Biff's new bubble machine.

'This is great fun,' shouted Wilf.

'Yeah,' cried Wilma.

Just then the magic key began to glow.

'We're off somewhere,' said Chip.

They were spinning round and round until they fell on the floor with a bump. They stood up, they were in a zoo. Then they saw something very strange indeed, a monkey that sounded like a lion.

As they walked around all the animals were making the wrong noises. They saw the zookeeper and Wilf asked, 'Why are your animals making the wrong noises?'

'The magic cat swapped the voices round. Can you help me to find the cat?'

'Of course,' everybody shouted.

They started looking, then Chip spotted it. He crept upon it and grabbed it, then all the animals had their own voice again and the cat disappeared.

The magic key started to glow.

'Thanks,' shouted the zookeeper.

'Any time,' said Chip and they went back home.

Alice Blain (8)
Newlands Community Primary School

HOW THE SNAKE GOT TO BE ORANGE

One day the snake was blue and had red stripes, but he decided he wanted to be orange with blue stripes, so he went to the beach and found a magic potion.

On the bottle it said *only to be used if you've got blue skin and red stripes and are a snake.*
'Yes!' so he drank up the potion and he felt funny and he started to sing, 'Zapay do - zapy do - dapey do.' He turned brown, then white, then red, then finally orange with blue stripes. 'Yes it worked!' said the snake.

He went back to show his friends and he always felt special from that day on.

Sam Hyde (8)
Newlands Community Primary School

How The Giraffe Got His Long Neck

Gerry Giraffe was going on holiday, not a summer holiday. No she was going to the jungle to meet her friend. But there was just one thing that Gerry was worrying about, she didn't know what to eat. She'd forgotten to bring some food (she thought more about her hats' than food).

Luckily she saw some fruits on the trees but they were too high up. Just then a snake slithered on her best hat so Gerry grabbed the snake and ate it whole. All the animals were scared of her. Her neck grew longer and longer and from that day on that was how she was.

Sophie Halliwell (9)
Newlands Community Primary School

THE GHOST HOUSE

'Lisa! It's time to go to your uncle Paul's house,' shouted Mum. 'You don't want to be late.'

Lisa scurried downstairs as fast as she could. Lisa couldn't wait to get into Uncle Paul's mansion!

Lisa looked around the enormous house looking for Uncle Paul. The house seemed to be strange. Then suddenly, 'Boo! Ha! Scared you didn't I?'

'Uncle Paul you scared the socks off of me!' Lisa screamed.

'Come on Lisa, I'll show you the room you will be staying in.'

Lewis Betts (11)
Newlands Community Primary School

THE HOUSE ON THE HILL

Christopher was eating his lunch. When he got home his mum said, 'We're moving house.'

'Yes,' shouted Chris, 'we're moving house!'

Chris went upstairs to pack his bags. He kept saying to himself, 'Yes, we're moving house, yes we're moving house!' Chris was so excited he was moving house the next day. 'It will be great, with the big old door and the old brown windows.'

'OK, lights off! We've got a big day tomorrow,' called his mum.

'Yes,' shouted Chris as he got out of bed. 'We're moving house.' Then Chris ran down the stairs asking his mum when they were going to move.

'Two o'clock,' replied Mum.

'Can I go and say bye to Ben then Mum?'

'OK but be back for one o'clock.'

'OK Mum,' replied Chris.

Chris went to say bye to Ben. While he was there he had one last go on his PlayStation 2.

It was time to go and with only fifteen minutes to get home he had to run all the way. When he got home his mum and dad were already packing the van. When they left it was a half an hour journey to the house. Finally they arrived outside the house.

'Yes, the house is wicked,' shouted Chris. 'I can't wait to go inside. It will be great.'

'OK you can go in now,' said his mum.

Chris went into the house to take some boxes down to the basement when he slipped through a trapdoor and was bitten by what he thought was a poisonous snake.

Matthew Hutchinson (11)
Newlands Community Primary School

THE SPOOKY HOUSE

'Mum, Mum have you got everything?' said Jody. They were moving into their new house in the woods. The whole family were really excited. They set off on their journey.

That night everyone was very tired so they all went to bed. All of a sudden . . . *bang!* There was a noise coming from the basement. The two children went into their mum and dad's room looking very scared.
'Dad, Dad, go and have a look!' said Jody.
Dad went and had a look.
'Nothing was there,' he said. Then there was another bang. Mum said it must have been a cat.

In the morning they unpacked everything.

While they were eating their dinner Dad heard footsteps going down the stairs. Everyone was very scared because of the banging that night and the footsteps. Something was very strange. Mum contacted the previous owners. All of a sudden the light turned off and on. The people who lived there before said they moved away because they heard funny noises.

All night and all day they stayed up waiting for the noises to stop. They sold the house in the woods and went to live in a calmer, more loving house which was not in the woods.

Gemma Stone (11)
Newlands Community Primary School

FAIRY LAND WITH THE MAGIC CARPET

One day Chip was going to go to his gran's for the day while Mum was at work. Chip loved his gran, she played blocks with him when he was little and they went to the movies together. When Chip got to his gran's she had an old rug out.

'What is that old rug Gran?'

'My old play toy when I was little, it can fly.'

'But maybe the magic has gone because it's so old?'

'Good job I brought my magic key so we could fly.'

Great they both thought.

They waved goodbye to Mum and started brushing the old mat down and put some cushions on and food. Off they went up into the sky, moving slowly. It looked lovely, you could see your house from there. Gran looked at the sky map and saw a place called Fairy Land.

'Head straight forward, then you will get there,' said Gran. They went straight through the sign and found a parking space. It was lovely, you could see a fairy taking you through the history of fairies and how they made magic ages ago.

After they had had lunch and went to the magic fairy, you were allowed three wishes each. Chip made a wish that he could have another cat, that his mum would teach him to do some tricks and the last, to give money to the poor. Gran just wanted to have one wish and that was to stop people killing animals.

They decided to go home to see Mum but just before they left they went in the gift shop and bough a little fairy.

'That's all,' said Chip and went home to put the statue in a place so that it reminded them of the time they went to Fairy Land.

Amy Armitage (8)
Newlands Community Primary School

CHIP, KIPPER AND BIFF GO BACK IN TIME TO THE CASTLES

One day Kipper and Chip were playing on their Game Boys when the key started to glow brighter and brighter. Kipper and Chip disappeared, then they were at Nottingham Castle.

Then along came . . . Biff.
'What are you doing here?' said Chip.
'I've come to find you,' said Biff. 'That's all.'
They all wandered into the ghost tower where it had been haunted for many years. Chip was scared, so was Biff but they had Kipper to lead them in. As they walked on it got scarier and scarier, creepier and creepier, colder and colder, then . . . they . . . all . . . ran for it.
'Aarrgghh,' they all screamed,.
'I want to go home,' said Biff.
'So do I,' said Kipper.
'I don't,' said Chip.
They all sat down, then the guards came and put them in the dungeon.
'Now look what the key's done,' said Biff.
'Shut up!' said Kipper.
'Be quiet, I'm trying to think of a plan,' said Chip.
'Oh boy,' said Biff.

The guards came and they were just about to be hung when the key began to glow. They disappeared and were back at home safe and sound.
'Boy oh boy, I'm glad I'm home,' said Chip.
'We are!' shouted Kipper and Biff.'
'Personally I wouldn't like to be hanged,' said Biff.
'Me either,' said Kipper and Chip!

Abbie Hutchinson (8)
Newlands Community Primary School

HOW THE GIRAFFE GOT ITS LONG NECK

One day in the jungle there was a giraffe. He had a very short neck, his mother was very ashamed of him, so she named him Shorty. When he went to school everyone laughed at him so he went to the headmaster, but he was not there so he went home to his mum.

'I wish I didn't have such a short neck.'

'Don't worry dearest, you're my son.'

The next day he went to school even though everyone was laughing. He did not take any notice of them.

Today was a test, everyone was still laughing. He got an A plus, 'Well done Shorty, excellent you are promoted up to Grade A.'

'Oh my goodness I don't know what to say.'

'Don't say anything.'

He rushed home to tell his mum the good news. 'Mum, Mum guess what just happened?'

'What?'

'I got promoted up to Grade A.'

His mum was gobsmacked, she did not know what to do.

'Well done Shorty, I am very pleased for you. I hope you get on well in your new school. Let's have a celebration party.'

His mum called all her friends for a celebration and they had a party. 'Congratulations Shorty.'

James Mangham (9)
Newlands Community Primary School

HOW THE SNAKE GOT NO LEGS

A long time ago snakes had 20 legs and were the fastest animals in the world. One day a snake called Fred was walking through the jungle singing a song. 'Dee dum, dee dum, dee dum,' he sang. Then a dinosaur crashed through the trees. 'Oh no not you again,' said Fred, who had escaped this dinosaur 9 times already. This time he was mad.
'I want my dinner,' he said.
'Yeah, well you're not getting any, that mouse is doing perfectly well in my belly,' shouted Fred.

Then Fred pretended to be the mouse. 'Yes I'm OK so get stuffed,' he said squeakily.

The dinosaur looked angry so Fred dashed off, but the dinosaur caught him and bit off ten of his legs. While the dinosaur was munching Fred's legs, Fred slithered off.

In the future Fred still existed but he had human predators. They caught him and stripped off the rest of his legs so he couldn't escape. He was put on a kebab. Then a human bit his tail so no skin was left. The human's teeth marks were left in his bone.

He slithered away with no legs. He didn't taste very nice. Fred is now a snake with no legs.

Bailey Drescher (9)
Newlands Community Primary School

HOW THE TURTLE GOT HIS SHELL

One day it was very hot so a turtle went down to the sea to cool down. He was swimming along in the sea when all of a sudden a shell floated across and stuck to his back. He got out of the sea to try to get it off, but he couldn't.

It was getting hotter, so he curled inside the shell. It was cool inside so he stayed in there until the sun was going down. When he tried to crawl out he couldn't and that is how the turtle got his shell.

Charlotte Stubbs (8)
Newlands Community Primary School

THE WICKED STEPMOTHER

'Jo, where's Dad?'

'Outside. Don't go out there Gemma.'

'Why, what are you going to do? Smack me?'

'No!'

'I'm glad that you're not my mother,' said Gemma, 'you're only a step one, so don't forget that.'

When they all went off to bed her stepmother Jo set traps all around the house. The next morning Gemma woke up and walked into the kitchen. She walked into a piece of string, a metal thing fell from the ceiling, it was a cage.

Her dad ran down the stairs to see where the noise was coming from. He got stuck in some rope.

The stepmother told the rules to them. She took all of their money and when Gemma's real mother arrived to give the keys back, she went in. She took Gemma and her dad out and they rang the police.

The wicked stepmother was caught by the police, she was sent to prison. Gemma asked her mother if she wanted to stay for a night or two. They were playing games all night, they had so much fun that she stayed for a week.

Her grandma came round and stayed for dinner and they loved it. Her grandma stayed for two weeks because she lived in Scotland and that was a long, long way. Gemma loved it when her mother visited.

Charlie Mayne (11)
Newlands Community Primary School

How Did The Snakes Get Their Forked Tongues?

One day there was some snakes called Hissey, Hiss and Hisster. No snakes in the world had a forked tongue. Hissey, Hiss and Hisster lived in Australia. They liked it there because they had some friends called Elephant and Monkey. They were the best friends they had ever had.

They all decided to ask Elephant how they all could get a forked tongue. Elephant said, 'Sorry, I can't help you.'
So they all went to Monkey and said, 'Can you help us?'
'Sorry no I can't,' he said.

They all knew the wise lion would know what to do so one day they all went to find him. They all split up to find him. Then Hiss found him and shouted, 'I've found him,' and they rushed over.
Hissey went up to say something but he was too scared so Hisster went up and said, 'Can you help us get a forked tongue?' He showed him his tongue and the lion bit it into a forked tongue.

Hissey went up and said, 'Can you help us get a forked tongue?' and he showed him his tongue and the lion bit his tongue so then it was a forked tongue.

All the other snakes went up and he bit into their tongues so they were forked tongues and that was how the snakes got their forked tongues.

Gemma Wale (9)
Newlands Community Primary School

WHY SNAKE HAS NO LEGS

Snake has legs and walks. He has four legs like most other animals. Snake has a dream, his dream is to jump! One day Snake decides to try. Snake finds a tree and climbs up but is too scared to jump.

He sets off again and finds some rocks. He climbs the rocks and doesn't notice a bear is sleeping behind them. Then Snake accidentally wakes up the bear. The bear chases Snake, but Snake gets away. Snake stops to rest but the bear finds him.

As soon as Snake realises he jumps to his feet but then he comes to a cliff and he has to jump but is too scared. Snake plucks up his courage and jumps . . . and when he hits the bottom he lands on his legs and his legs get squashed into his body and that is why snake have no legs.

Laura Rowley (9)
Newlands Community Primary School

HOW LEOPARDS GET SPOTS

Once upon a time there lived a young leopard who was jealous about not having patterns on his fur so he said to his mum, 'I want a pattern on my fur.'

So his mum replied, 'Oh you will, you will!'

Leopard was really excited. The next day he said to Turtle, 'I will get a pattern.'

'Wow!' said Turtle.

So Leopard rolled in the mud to get a pattern and rushed home and shouted, 'Look at my new pattern Mother!'

'You little devil, that no pattern, that's a spill! I will wash you to see if it is a pattern.'

Mother Leopard scrubbed all over, but the mud washed off. Mother Leopard said, 'That's no pattern, just a spill!'

So Leopard's next attempt was rolling in blackberries, which he did. Then he ran back home, 'Mum, I have a pattern.'

'Let's wash it,' said Mother Leopard. She scrubbed and rubbed but the pattern wouldn't come off. 'That's a pattern,' shouted Mother Leopard and from that day forward leopards far and wide rolled in berries to get a pattern.

Jack Leman (9)
Newlands Community Primary School

HOW CAT GOT HER PURR

In the middle of the Mediterranean Sea on the beautiful island of Lesbos, lived a cat called Claudia. She was lovely and white as a fluffy snowball. Although she was beautiful, she had a problem, she couldn't purr or rather, she didn't know how to purr. Claudia had two friends, one was a coconut-coloured monkey called Mia and the other was a golden Labrador called Lulu, the colour of the sand on the isle of Lesbos.

Claudia was playing with her friends on the beach. She was doing acrobatics while Mia and Lulu were flicking water at each other. They were so happy frolicking around, the sun was shining like a golden fireball. The sky was bright blue and looked bare because it showed not one cloud. Claudia stopped doing her acrobatics and looked at her friends playing. She felt so happy and contented, when all of a sudden she felt a noise coming from her throat.

Claudia couldn't believe it, she gambolled and flipped in the air she could purr and every time she was happy she started to purr.

Rosanna Chamberlain (9)
Newlands Community Primary School

WHY THE SHEEP IS WOOLLY

Sheep was a happy sheep. Apart from one thing, he was cold. So he decided that he would go and look for a way to keep himself warm. So off he went.

Sheep tried staying in a small cave. He thought an enclosed space would keep him warm. But as he went into the cave he heard a growling noise. *A bear!* Sheep ran away as quickly as he could. He didn't want to stay in there! He tried covering himself in leaves. That didn't work either.

Sheep was sad, he felt as if he would never be warm again. As Sheep walked along he heard a human talking. Sheep went to see what the human was talking about. When the human noticed him she saw he was sad. 'What's wrong?' she asked.
'I'm cold,' Sheep replied.
The lady gave Sheep a woolly jumper. 'That will keep you warm,' she said.
Sheep thanked the lady and ran off. He loved his jumper so much he never took it off. And he still wears it now.

Eleanor Davies (9)
Newlands Community Primary School

THE CHOCOLATE FACTORY

One day Biff, Chip, Kipper and Anneena were playing, but suddenly the magic key started to glow. 'Goody, goody,' said Anneena, 'I wonder where we will go?' The children were amazed at where they ended up.
'Wow! We're in a chocolate factory,' shouted Biff.
'Hello, I am Ken, champion of making chocolate.'

First Ken showed them the caramel room. 'Wow,' shouted Chip, 'I love caramel.'
All the children got a taste, but Chip had the most. 'Here is my ice cream machine,' said Ken.
Kipper got covered in ice cream.

'When we get back we'll have to clean you up,' said Anneena.
'Last of all the chocolate maker,' shouted Ken.

All the children loved chocolate. 'You can all have a taste if you like,' said Ken.
When they had all got their piece of chocolate the key began to glow.
'Time to clean you up,' said Anneena.

When they got back Kipper said, 'That chocolate is better than the chocolate from the shops.'

Dexter Jeffries (8)
Newlands Community Primary School

HOW THE SUN WAS MADE

Once there were four children, the first one was called Dan, the second was called Ben, the third was called Joe and the last one was called Ashley.

The four friends were blowing a big bubble. They watched it rise up into the sky when suddenly ten meteorites crashed into a comet, a missile crashed into the comet too. They all crashed into a planet and the bubble exploded. The pieces of bubble caught fire and spread all over the planet. They never did it again.

Ashley Forman (9)
Newlands Community Primary School

HOW THE CAMEL GOT HER HUMPS

Many years ago, in a jungle, there lived a camel, gorilla and kangaroo and their babies. The jungle was very grassy, muddy and full of trees with vines hanging down. The gorilla found it easy to get around the jungle by swinging on the trees. The kangaroo went round by jumping, but kept hitting her head on the tree branches and the camel slowly plodded along getting her feet caught in the long grasses.

The baby animals needed help to get around so the gorilla let her baby climb on her back. The kangaroo had a handy pocket for her baby, but the camel had a problem. The friends thought about tying a vine round her middle and her baby would hang on.

This worked until the baby got bigger then it was too heavy. When the baby camel was older he plodded on his own. The camel took off the vine and because of the heavy baby she was left with a big dip in her back. It looked like she had two humps.

The camel said to her friends she couldn't carry her baby like that again. The friends said she needed to live somewhere else. They thought of the desert where it was soft and flat. The only problem was there was not a lot of water there. The camel said she could use her new humps to keep water in and it would last for days. The camel and her baby set off and lived happily ever after and still do today.

Evan Marshalsey (9)
Newlands Community Primary School

THE STORY BOOK

One day Biff, Chip, Wilf, Wilma, Kipper and Anneena were playing in the back garden at football and on their bikes. They were racing around and suddenly . . . Biff, Kipper and Chip fell off their bikes. Wilf, Wilma and Anneena helped them up off the ground and they said, 'Are you all right?'

Then the key glowed, 'We're going somewhere,' said Biff. 'Where?'

'Inside the book called Peter Pan, let's see if we can see him.'

'Argh! There he is. Hello Peter Pan,' said Chip.

'Hello,' said Peter Pan.

'Can you take us through the book please?' said Wilf.

'Yes, I'd be glad to.'

'Good, let's go . . . are you sure Wilf? This place looks creepy.'

'Yes, I'm sure, it's just your imagination.'

'Yes, OK.'

'Well, are we going to start yet?'

'Yes!'

Teeee, teeee, teeeee, teeee, teeee.

'That's it, it's the whole book.'

'Just in time, the key's starting to glow.'

'See you, Peter Pan.'

'See you.'

They got home and went round Chip's house to have a drink of hot chocolate. I wonder where they will go next, do you?

Laurie Grewcock (8)
Newlands Community Primary School

SHINY LAND

One morning Chip, Kipper and Anneena were playing outside. Chip had the magic key. Chip, Kipper and Anneena were playing football in the back garden. Then the magic key began to glow. Chip said to Kipper and Anneena, 'Where are we going this time?'

'We don't know, do we! Well here we go, *whheeee*. We're here, we're here. Wait, don't, no, it's so bright. I can already see!'

'Here you are, some dark glasses.'

'Thanks Anneena. I think we're in Shiny Land. Remember on the TV they said there's a new place!'

'Oh yeah, we're there. Wow!'

'My mum wouldn't let me go there because it's too far away.'

'My mum said we could go next week, but we're here already, so when I go next week I can tell my mum all about it, can't I!'

'Yes, you can. I wish I could go again!'

'Look at that moon, it's really bright and shiny,' said Anneena.

'Do you want to go outside in Shiny Land's back garden?'

'This is shiny too?' said Kipper.

'Yes it is, isn't it!' said Anneena.

'This is great! Do you want to ask that man if he can swap us £3 for £2?'

'Yeah, come on!'

'Excuse me.'

'Yes?'

'Can you swap us £3 and we will give you £2?'

'No!'

'Run! Come on Anneena, run faster, he is catching up with us.'

Then the key began to glow. 'We're going home, *whheeee!'*

'We're here. Hi Mum!'

'I've been shouting you for dinner.'

OK, sorry, bye Anneena, bye Chip!'

Laura Hill (7)
Newlands Community Primary School

HOW ELEPHANT GOT HIS LONG TRUNK

One day Elephant was walking along the path when he saw his friend Little Bear. Bear was a very clever bear and Elephant was not so clever because he didn't look as smart as Bear. Elephant had big, stompy feet and a very short trunk. Elephant lived in Africa and Bear lived in the rocks, so Elephant was very dusty and Bear was very well groomed. They were very different.

That afternoon Elephant was hungry so he decided to go and get something to eat. But then he could not reach the leaves at the top of the tree because his trunk was too short.

So he decided to stand on some rocks. But he fell off the rocks. The animals laughed. Elephant was very sad, so he went home and slept in until he heard some animals calling him.

Elephant went to the tree and all the animals were there and his other friend, the other elephant, didn't mind if he didn't have a long trunk. Then, all of a sudden, there was a rope around his trunk and the other elephant pulled on the tope and Elephant's trunk was very long. And now he can eat at the top of the trees. And that's how an elephant got his long trunk.

Jade Armstrong (9)
Newlands Community Primary School

THE ZOO

One day Chip, Biff and Kipper were having a game of Twister and the key started glowing. So they ran upstairs and went through the doll's house. They found themselves in a zoo, so they had a look around.

First, they went to see the monkeys. Then they went to see the elephants and they got squirted by one! Biff and Kipper couldn't find Chip. They looked at the ice cream van, at the lions, at the tigers, at the monkeys, at the rhinos, at the hippos, even at the giraffes, but he was nowhere to be found.

They called all the people at the zoo to the monkey house and asked them if they had seen a little boy and they looked in the crowd but he wasn't there. Then all the elephants came charging at them and they ran, ran, ran, ran, and ran until they were all worn out. The elephants ran on to the road and everybody chased them apart from Biff and Kipper. They went and looked for Chip in the snake area and they found him.

So they helped to catch the elephants and they caught them. Then the adventure ended. 'Well, that was fun!' said Chip.
'Yes it was,' said the others, 'that was a good adventure.'

Matthew Kerr (8)
Newlands Community Primary School

WORLD WAR I

Once there lived a girl called Biff, a boy called Chip and a boy called Kipper. They had a magic key which shone when they had an adventure. 'Biff, have we got an adventure?' asked Kipper.
'For the last time, no,' replied the other two.
'Why?'
'Because the key isn't shining. Hang on a minute, it is.'
Suddenly a door appeared.
'Let's go,' said Biff.

So they ran in. There was a huge *bang!* A bullet went whizzing past them. 'Where are we?' asked Kipper.
'We're in World War I,' replied Chip.
'A war, did you say?'
'Yes, I did.'

Suddenly a man came running down the battlefield. His name was Sir Ellis. 'This is no place for little children.' Suddenly a bullet went through Sir Ellis. He fell back dead.

Next a man called Jack came. 'Watch out!' shouted Jack. 'Argh!' Jack was now dead.
'Quick,' said a man called Lewis.
Yes, Lewis had shot a German.
Kaboom! Lewis was hit by a bomb.

A noble and brave man called Laurie got them back to safety and the magic key took them back to their house. But they had a helmet with them.

Lewis Grewcock (8)
Newlands Community Primary School

THE GENIE

Once there lived a girl called Biff and boys called Chip and Kipper.
They were all in bed when Kipper was on his Zombie game. Suddenly
the key started to glow. 'Biff, Chip, come quickly,' shouted Kipper.
They ran into Kipper's room. *Bang!* They all landed in an adventure.

There, right in front of them Kipper found a magic lamp. It was dirty,
so he decided to rub it. *Kaboom!* A magic genie!
'Woooo,' said Biff and Chip.
'I am the genie of the lamp. I can give you three wishes and that is what
I grant you.'
'I wish I had a gun,' said Chip.
'Your wish is my command.'
'Cool,' said Chip in a surprised voice.

The others started to wish too. *Bang! Bang! Bang!* The bats flew away,
out of the dark cave.
'Wow, that was naughty,' said Kipper.
'Er, oh no, the key's started glowing again!'
Biff, Chip and Kipper were back home and they never played with guns
again.

Jack Orton (8)
Newlands Community Primary School

THE HOUSE OF THE DEAD

I glanced out of the window, gazing at the house. I could see a dusty, meandering brick pathway leading to the crooked oak door belonging to the dilapidated, shabby, lifeless and vast house. There were huge strands of ivy creeping up the oak door, like a gate unwelcoming a guest. I could see a neglected garden with flowers shrivelled and petalless. On top of the roof there stood a stone gargoyle. The house had caught me in a trace that I could not wake up from . . .

I found myself in front of the vast house. I crept up to the oak door. Suddenly, when I was one step away from the house, the door gradually started to open. I analysed the insides, something moved in the pure, dingy darkness. Slowly, but steadily, I made my way in. Inside a light flickered. A cobweb brushed against my face. I stifled a scream, but nothing came out. In I walked, further and further.

I had the feeling I was being watched. I stood motionless. *Stay calm, stay calm,* I told myself. Something or someone came in after me, I couldn't think of anything else but to run. I scrambled to the door. Suddenly, the door barred itself. I skidded to a halt. *Oh no I'm trapped,* I thought.

I stared into a grimy mirror. There was a door swinging in the wind. I tiptoed in. It was a kitchen. The pots and pans were washing themselves. I walked onto a silk rug. Suddenly I found myself sliding down a chute. I'd fallen through a trapdoor. It was a long trip. Finally, I found myself in a small room with spiders scuttling across the floor. It was the *cellar!* It was dark and dingy and the bricks were polluted with filthy water. It was almost like a sewer. It was then that I heard it. A dripping, scratching sound. I leaned against the wall and suddenly a door opened. There was a staircase leading upwards . . .

I marched up. A shadow shifted. I was so frightened I nearly fell back down the staircase. It took me back to where I started, in the hall of the house. I crept off looking for something hard. I snuck up another set of stairs. I opened a door which had a shovel inside. *Just what I was looking for . . .*

I went back down the stairs. I used the shovel to make a tunnel which led out of the house. I kept digging and digging until I was out of the house. 'Hooray!' I yelled. But the gate was closed. I noticed a wall and climbed over it to get free of the house.

Thomas Brant (8)
The Latimer School

BEWARE OF THE GHOST STORY

The timber door screeched open as I peered into the dark, dilapidated house. I stepped forward onto rickety floorboards. There were ripped curtains and smashed windows all around the place. The house made me feel sick. I thought it was a dream, but it wasn't a dream.

I had to go in, I just had to, even though the sign said not to. I had to go in, I just had to. I tried to run, but I couldn't.

Shaun Cole (9)
The Latimer School

THE HOUSE OF THE DEAD

As I looked out of the window my gaze fell on the crumbling stone pathway leading to the dilapidated house. It towered above all the other houses. The garden was neglected and the flowers were shrivelling up. Even the daisies looked as if no one had cared for them. Ivy was creeping up the weather-beaten bricks. Howling wind battled against the broken windows. Above the cracking chimney, thunder rolled and lightning flickered. I didn't dare go in. But I knew I had to . . .

The rusty, oak door creaked open and I found myself stepping inside. I cautiously took a few steps forward, then I froze. I thought I saw a yellow eye swivelling in the darkness. I felt feathers brush past my face. I stifled a scream. I suddenly felt something sharp and pointed stick into my cheek. I mopped my stinging cheek with a hanky and when I removed it, there was blood all over it.

I stared up into the filthy, grimy mirror before me. *Oh no,* I thought, *it couldn't be, it can't be . . .*

It was then that I heard it. A scratching, scraping sound. It came from behind the mirror. I turned to run, but my way was barred.

Holly Woolveridge (8)
The Latimer School

THE HAUNTED FOREST

I was walking through the forest with my friend. I saw two more of my friends were stuck at the end of the forest with thorns holding them back. We knew we had to help them.

We chopped the thorns as we were on our way to the exit. A man had barred the thorns as it was too dangerous for kids to go in there. So he barred the way.

All four of us were trapped inside the forest. Luckily we found a hole in-between two trees. But before we went through the hole we saw an army of ghosts . . .

Lauren Helps (9)
The Latimer School

THE DILAPIDATED COTTAGE

I gazed across the pebbled and crumbly road. The smell was foul, I couldn't stand it. I shut my window and put my dressing gown on and went. It was cold outside but because the cottage had hypnotised me I did not notice because I was too interested in the cottage . . .

I am going in the cottage now. I am pushing the door. The door is squeaking on one rusty, old hinge. Finally, I get in the cottage and look around, cobwebs and rats are scattered all over the place. I step into the living room, there is old Victorian furniture. I tiptoe into the kitchen, stoves are still on. I know someone is in here . . .

Suddenly, *bang!* The door slams shut. It makes me jump out of my skin. I can see the curly wurly stairs. I go up step by step. I go into the bathroom. I can see something move behind the shower curtain. I want to scream but I don't because I am too scared. I think I know what it is - a ghost.

The ghost starts to chase me, I am near the door, but my way is barred. Suddenly the door flies open . . .

Chelsea Etchells (7)
The Latimer School

LOCKED

I blinked back tears as I gazed out of my attic window. I could see a large house. At first I thought it was haunted and then it struck me, maybe those old stories were true. So I thought of running downstairs to my mum, who was comfortably lying on the sofa. Why? I was strong, I could do it. I did not dare go in, but I knew I had to . . .

I found myself one-on-one with the timber door of the dilapidated house. I stepped forward three steps. Then when I had he courage to, I gradually pushed open the door. I walked into an art gallery. I saw eyes moving on the portrait. I stifled a scream, as I made my way into the next room. Before I could get there, something or someone hit me hard on my back. I didn't know what it was, but I knew I had to leave, but then the door shut . . .

'Show yourself now!' I bellowed at the something or someone.
I heard a voice saying, 'You will find the key under one particular floorboard and be warned, ha, ha, ha!' the voice sniggered. *What's that?* I wondered as I stared at the strange shape. I crept forward.
'It's a metal detector!' I did look surprised. I switched it on and used it. After a while it started beeping, then I came to a floorboard and it beeped fast. I ripped up the floorboard and finally I found the key to the door and escaped.

When I got out, the gate was locked . . .

Greg Elsom (8)
The Latimer School

THE HOUSE OF HAUNTED PEOPLE

I gazed out of the window, peering at the dilapidated house. I could see a meandering, stony pathway leading to a creaky door that only had one hinge. It was swinging back and forth, back and forth, back and forth, I shut the curtains and then heard a noise! Something like a door opening and then closing. I opened the curtains and saw that somebody had gone in the house and I thought I knew who. I had to go in, I had to!

I found myself in front of the lounge looking around at the portraits. Their eyes were moving, I nearly screamed but I knew I couldn't. I paused for a few minutes, it was frightening but I had to find the person who had strolled in. I carried on walking, then I heard a noise like footsteps following me. I looked around - there was nothing. I carried on again. It was dark, there were no lights, they kept switching on and off. I heard something upstairs, I gripped on to the stair banister and I slowly walked up.

I looked into a bedroom, nothing there and when I went into the bathroom something hit me and suddenly a shadow was following me as I was walking. I went into another bedroom. I found blood on a knife next to an old friend. I tried to get out but the door was locked. I couldn't get out, I was trapped. The room started to overheat like a fire starting. I shouted, 'Help, somebody help!' Nothing. I kept on repeating it. Somebody came and looked into the bedroom I was in and saw that nothing was there. The heat then increased and burst into flames.

Jessica Carter (9)
The Latimer School

RETURN NEVER COMES

I had a nightmare. I got up and glanced out of the window casting my sleepy eyes on the pummelled and battered house across the street. There was a jagged, meandering pathway leading to an oak door which was swinging on one rusty, old hinge. On top of the door was a hideous gargoyle. Ivy was slowly creeping up the walls. The house was neglected and shabby. The curtains were tatty and ripped and flapped like birds' wings.

At the rear of the property the garden was overgrown with dead weeds and long, wild grass. It was dark and cold and sad and lonely. There were two trees both bent, alone and bare. There was an unpleasant smell in the windy breeze. I couldn't take my eyes off the house, I had to go in, I just had to . . .

I started to get dressed. I crept down the stairs. I crossed the street to the house. Thunder was pounding in the wind, lightning was crackling down like magic. I crunched my way up the driveway to the overgrown house. I clutched the doorknob tightly. It gradually opened. All the other houses were pretty compared to this overgrown ivy house. I tiptoed and stepped in, the door slammed behind me, *thud!*

I was in the great hall. I glanced around. It looked like a ruin. There were mysterious pictures on the walls. There were some stairs to the left and the right, leading to rooms. I took a step further. Rats were scuttling on the floorboards, hole to hole. An eye moved on one of the pictures, *suspicious* I told myself, *I'm not alone!* I heard footsteps . . .

I strolled up the stairs to the attic and fastened the door.
'Oooooooohh!' said a voice.
'Wh-wh-who is it?' I mumbled. I looked around there was silence.

A spirit rose up. I was gobsmacked. I turned to run but I couldn't move. I stood motionless, stuck to the ground.

'Don't worry. I'm a friendly spirit,' he howled. 'I will help you on your way.' I looked around. I tiptoed down to the bathroom, the mirror was smashed with bloodstains. The bath was smashed in half and the tap was running, *plip-plop, plip-plop*. I went into the bedroom. The bed had skulls on the corners. I started walking, library books were on the floor with a bookshelf on the floor. I looked out of the haunted house, I saw my house, but haunted.

Jamie Skipper (9)
The Latimer School

The Haunted House

I saw the wild garden behind the rusty gate. It had irises peeking over and under the overgrown, dead grass. I accidentally stepped on a watering can which sent spiders scuttling in and out.

I gradually opened the front door. I went in. As soon as I stepped inside it got darker and darker with every footstep. Then I heard a large *bang!* I saw staircases leading up to some doors that had not been opened for years. There was a key on the top shelf. I clutched the key so hard, I didn't dare go in, but I knew I had to . . .

My hand was shaking. The key got closer to the keyhole. I opened the door. Cobwebs brushed past my face. A man bellowed, 'You will find a key on your next adventure.'
'Wh-wh-what adventure?' I cried.
'Your adventure to find the forbidden key. I will help you though.'

I heard a scratching sound behind the front door. I stifled a scream. But nothing came out.
'Heh, the key is under the floorboard.'
I ran downstairs and opened the front door. I ran to open the gate and it was locked . . .

Joshua Brian (9)
The Latimer School

THE HOUSE OF DOOM

I pulled back the curtains and gazed across the crumbling road towards my nightmare! The neglected, dilapidated cottage had a cold and angry look. The windows were rusty and cracked, the garden had overgrown weeds, the path had loose bricks and there was a dark forest nearby that no one dared to enter.

The house looked haunted and I didn't dare go in. But I knew I had to. The door's hinges were smashed, the floorboards were loose. The windows were smashed. It made me want to get out of there. A cobweb brushed past my face as I ran to the bedroom door.

The door was locked. I ran to the window, it slammed shut with a *bang!* Fire shot out of the goblin's mouth as I ran. There were two swords stuck to the wall. I tried to move all of the junk . . . the house came tumbling down.

Charlie Southam (8)
The Latimer School

TERROR TIME

I shivered and gulped back tears, whilst analysing the meandering, stony pathway which led up to the most feared place in history. The moth-bitten, bare curtains fluttering like bats' wings in a terrible storm were flowing in and out of the shattered windows. I noticed an immense jungle-like garden, its overgrown grass was shrivelling up. Dandelions covered the broken fence. I could only hear a *howl!*

Before I knew it I was standing in front of a giant timber door which towered above me. I gave it a slight push, it swung open. I heard a giant scuttle along the broken floorboards which were stained with black, gooey slime that trailed up to the staircase made out of steel. This led to a set of oak doors.

My eyes widened, my heart thundered faster and faster. I inspected each creepy painting until I heard a hoarse voice say, *'Coommee mmyy pprreettyy, coommee.'* I wanted to run, but my legs turned to jelly.

Gradually I calmed down and took a few deep breaths. I ventured upstairs into the first oak door. The key was already in the lock, so I turned it. The oak door opened. Inside I saw what I thought was a dream. Two baby skeletons underneath a ragged, torn cloth. I walked in, my screams were stifled as an enormous knight with a sparkling sword plunged down on me. I opened one eye, then the other, the sword missed my head by an inch. 'I'm outta here,' I screamed, as I scrambled from underneath the knight.

I examined the skeletons, suddenly flesh began to grow on them. I nearly fainted as the babies began to *coo.* 'Mama, Dadda,' they babbled, as they began to crawl towards me. I ran out of the door as quick as a flash. I slammed the door shut and locked it behind me.

I slowly wandered down to the third floor and crept inside, but the door locked all by itself and a crooked, bony hand grabbed the key out of my grasp. A further eight bony hands took me and tied me up in chains and hung me from the top of the four-poster bed. The chains somehow squeezed tighter, my head flopped forward, the house went up in flames. My charred bones rattled like wind chimes in a subtle breeze.

Callan Reed (9)
The Latimer School

SPOOK HOUSE

I peered out of my bedroom window at the neglected and shabby house on the other side. The huge garden was overgrown with weeds and masses of ivy was slithering up the wall. The house was stained with mud and rain on the bricks. The windows were vandalised. Then I noticed the roof tiles. Most of them were missing.

I didn't dare go in. But I knew I had to . . . minutes later I was at the oak front door. I pushed the oak door, it gradually creaked open. I stumbled inside. A huge breeze brushed past my face. I stifled a scream. It started to get damp and the floorboards started to creak. I heard something move, I steadily gazed around, then carried on walking. Suddenly, the door slammed shut. *Get a grip,* I told myself.

A shadow shifted. Someone or something was in there with me . . . I turned around, everywhere was barred except for the stairs. I tiptoed my way up them. I made my way into a room, the door creaked shut. I tried to open it but someone had locked me in. I sat on the creaky, old bed. Once I was comfortable I nodded off to sleep.

The next day I woke up in my bedroom. I knew something weird was going on. Then I remembered my nightmare. I looked out of my bedroom window, or was it a nightmare?

Rebecca MacTaggart (8)
The Latimer School

DEATH COMES QUICKLY

I gazed out of the window and saw my worst nightmare. The most frightening house in the world. The garden was overgrown with weeds and the dead ivy was falling off the dilapidated walls. I saw the moth-eaten curtains flapping in the wind. The windows were smashed and broken. On the very top of the roof was the most monstrous gargoyle.

At the rear of the house there was a wooden door screeching in the wind, on one rusty, old hinge. The unpleasant stench made me feel sick, but I couldn't close the window. The house had hypnotised me. I had to go in, I just had to . . .

Minutes later I found myself in front of the timber door. It creaked open. I stepped inside. The door slammed shut behind me with a loud *bang!* I walked up to the creaky, wooden staircase. Something cold brushed past my face. I stifled a scream. It was then that I heard it. A scratching sound was coming from the door. Someone or something had locked it. I tried to get out but the doorknob burned my hand. 'Something very strange is going on here,' I muttered to myself. A mysterious feeling came to me. *I think someone is trying to keep me here.* I tried to run to the back door but my way was blocked.

Objects were floating around. I was really scared. I ran up to the attic and slammed the door behind me. All of a sudden I heard a voice, 'Hello my sweet, get ready to die!'
'Arrgh!'
I woke up. I sighed with relief.
'Phew it was a dream!'
I looked out of my window and saw *the house!*

Sandy Stevenson (9)
The Latimer School

THE DARK HORROR OF THE HAUNTED HOUSE

I peered through my bedroom window. I was looking at an old house. It was neglected, dilapidated and lifeless. It had stone gargoyles on the vast roof. The gardens were overgrown with weeds. It looked like the gardens had had a war and the weeds had won. I looked up at a window, bats were hanging from the curtains. One of the gargoyles was lying in the weeds because the wind had knocked it off the roof. Ivy was taking over the house. The house looked haunted. I would never go in! But I knew I had to go in . . .

I ran to the gate of the haunted house. The gate was unlocked, I strolled in and I ran to the old, oak door. When I got right in front of the door it gradually opened and I saw something run away from the light. I was not positive what it was. I stepped in. There was a suit of armour in the centre of the hall. I walked to a painting. I looked at it carefully. As I looked at the painting its eyes began to move. A shiver ran down my spine. I stepped back. The armour had gone. I smelled someone's breath. I looked to the side of me and there was the suit of armour with a sword. I ran to the door. Luckily it was open. But when I got to the gate, it was locked . . .

I ran round to the back of the house, there was another suit of armour. I got suited up. It had two swords beside it so I picked them up. As the suit of armour came round the corner I swung the swords at it. *Bang!* It was dead. Then all of a sudden a creature jumped over the gate and . . . ran into my house. So I chased it. There it was in my bedroom, in my bed. I killed it with the swords. That night I could not sleep.

Thomas Lett (9)
The Latimer School

THE HOUSE OF SPOOKS

I gazed out of my bedroom window and saw a house. One rusty hinge on the oak door was broken as it swung in the wind. Six of the windows were smashed, the weather-beaten bricks were stained with polluted water. I saw a meandering pathway leading to the entrance. Bricks were pushed out from the inside and I heard a scream. I was going into the house, but I was so scared I couldn't because I saw ivy slowly creeping up the walls. I could smell something worse than a fly, it came from the dilapidated chimney. I couldn't go in. But I just knew I had to.

I went into the house, I tiptoed up the meandering staircase. This led me to a door, I paused. I carried on walking to the door, I pushed. I tried ringing my mum but my phone didn't work.

In the house was a dusty mirror. As I went into the room a spider's web brushed past my face. I stifled a scream! Two eyes were watching me! I ran, I was going to get out. But my way back was barred . . .

I worried, my heart was pounding! I ran upstairs into the room again. I heard someone, so I quietly closed the door. I looked through the keyhole, I saw it, it went right into the room I was in. He knew I was there, it was then my chance to escape. When he went round the corner I crept downstairs.
'Who-who-who's there?' I was stunned.
Out of the window I saw another dilapidated house where my house had been. It was my house.

I gazed out of my bedroom window and saw a house. One rusty hinge on the oak door was broken also . . .

Bradley Ellicock (8)
The Latimer School

THE SPOOKIEST HOUSE ON EARTH

I blinked back tears as I gazed out of the window. I spotted, out of the corner of my eye, a meandering, stone pathway leading towards a neglected, dull front garden. The garden stood in front of a tall, dilapidated house. The ivy that had grown up the rusty side of the house was attached to some old trellis by two or three leaves. The chimney had become bent by the heavy wind.

The house looked haunted and I did not dare go in. But I knew I had to. Suddenly I found myself at the front of the tall, dilapidated house. Gradually the old, unpainted door creaked open. I took a small step inside. A piece of the moth-eaten curtains brushed past my cold face. I felt like I needed to scream. I tried to scream, but I couldn't. My heart started to thud, I could feel it, I knew I was being watched . . .

After a while I continued to be nervous. I took a few more steps into the house. At the side of me there was an old, creaky, spiral staircase. I thought to myself, *Shall I go up them or shall I not?* I wondered, but I knew I had to go up them . . .

A few minutes later I was halfway up the stairs. Eventually I got to the top. Ahead of me lay three old oak doors. Suddenly, one of the doors creaked open. I walked up to the first door, I took a small step into the door. I walked around, I spotted something. It was a baby's crib. I crept up to it, unexpectedly the crib started to rock. After it had gotten very fast I spotted a black wing of some sort. Then I saw a black body and feet. Within minutes it flew from the crib. At this point I couldn't see what it was, until it flew over the top of me, it was then that I saw it, it was a bat. I didn't notice what it was doing until I heard it, a click. It was the click of the door. The only place I could escape from was the window. I couldn't jump out, it would kill me.
What could I do?

Alexandra Burton (8)
The Latimer School

THE HAUNTED HOUSE

One evening Joe was bored so he called for Sally and Tom. He met
them at the park and Sally dared Tom and Joe to go in the haunted
house. They went through the gates and opened the door. They were
shaking, but Tom and Joe went in and it was very creepy.

The door shut.
Joe said to Tom, 'Don't worry, there might be a key somewhere.'
They looked for the key. Tom went upstairs and looked in an old
bedroom and at that moment the door opened and closed.
A ghost said, 'Tom!'
In the bedroom was the key.
'Grab the key,' said Joe.
'I can't reach, you try.'
'I can't get the hook.'
Then Tom got it. 'Yes!'
They ran down the stairs.
'Yes, it fits.'
Running out of the house they shouted, 'Yes, we are free.'
They pushed the big gates open and ran home.
'Mum, I got stuck in a haunted house!'
'Stop being silly and eat your dinner, it's getting cold.'

Ryan Swanwick (9)
The Latimer School

The Dead

I peered out of my finger-printed window and saw a dilapidated house that had an old rusty door that swung on one rotten rusty hinge. I wanted to go in but it looked too dark and gloomy, and a bit scary.

I saw a black dilapidated wall and then I saw a black, gloomy creature. It zoomed across the great hall. When I stepped forwards onto a creaky floorboard it made me jump and then I got a fright.

I wanted to go home but I couldn't because the door had locked by itself. 'I'm scared. I want to go home.' When I went back to the living room I saw a dilapidated hall. I saw a secret passageway. It was locked. Something was coming downstairs. 'Aargh! We're done for it!'

The ghost had seen me. He had rotten grey fingers. The door had unlocked itself again. I got outside. When I got onto the pebbly path my house was near.

I got home and got in bed. I woke up the next morning and I thought it was just a dream.

But it wasn't.

Megan Varnham Fisher (8)
The Latimer School

THE DILAPIDATED HOUSE

I gave a little push on the oak door. I stood still for a second and looked in. It was pitch-black. I stopped. I had no idea where I was going. I heard a creaking noise in the background. I paused for a minute. The roars echoed away. I carried on walking, but I slipped.

I went up the creaking staircase. I reached the top of the staircase. I saw someone or something shoot past me. I stifled a scream. I carried on walking and I came to a window. I looked out of the window across the road and my house was *dilapidated* . . .

The door slammed shut on me. I tried to open it but it would not open. I tried and tried and pulled and pulled but the door would not open.

I stifled a scream. I made no noise at all. I was thinking of a way to get out. I could not think of anything to get out, but I looked around the room and I found a key.

I got out of the stinky old room and made my way down the stairs. I saw the door and I was free.

Jake Truman (8)
The Latimer School

THE HOUSE OF MY FRIEND'S GHOST

I heard a howling noise, so I pulled back the curtains and saw a meandering path leading to a dilapidated house. Its door was hanging on by one rusty hinge. The garden was overgrown and full of weeds. I thought it needed cutting. Ivy was slowly creeping up the crumbling walls. The chimney was half fallen down. I thought I would open the window to listen to the noises, so I carefully opened the window and was met by a howling noise, bats swooping and flapping about and an owl going *tu-whit tu-whuu.* The house looked haunted and I did not dare go in, but I knew I had to!

Gradually the oak door creaked open. I took a step forward into the building. I gingerly began to look around. I was sure I saw a pair of eyes moving in the portrait opposite me. I was now frozen to the spot through complete fear as to what I was about to witness next. I saw a dark shadow move into the kitchen, my whole body was trembling, but I had to investigate. I crept upstairs and entered the room in front of me, as that is where I saw the dark shadow disappear. I carefully opened the bedroom door. I came face to face with the dark shadow. I reached for the light switch as quickly as I could. At the same time I closed my eyes tight and held my breath. Then I gathered all my courage and strength. 'Who . . . who's there?' I muttered.
'Me!' said a voice, then my friend came out of the darkness.
'What are you doing here, Jess?'
'I came to your house to see if you were in here.'
Then we both saw more shadows moving around. We held hands as we began to move around the house trying to find out who was making these shadows. All of a sudden I felt very strange, but where was Jess?
I screamed, 'Jess, where are you?'
'In here,' Jess replied.
I entered the kitchen to find Jess shaking uncontrollably with a bloodstained knife in her hand and at her feet was her pet cat.
'Jess, what have you done?'

When I took a closer look, it wasn't my friend Jess standing there, but a scarecrow. I felt a strong push from behind. I fell forward into the cupboard. I heard the door slam and the key was turned in the lock.

The last thing I remembered as I drifted asleep was the smell of smoke. In my head I wondered what I had done to Jess for her to be so cruel to me.

Emily Llewellyn (9)
The Latimer School

TRAPPED

As I peered out of my bedroom window I saw the house that everyone had been going on about. It looked haunted. I couldn't go in but I knew I had to . . .

I thought it was just a normal house but I was wrong, it was more than that. The house was neglected and shadowy. 'It has to be lifeless,' I said to myself. The windows were so dirty you could only just see through them. The front door was swinging on one unnailed rusty hinge. The front garden was overgrown with weeds. I didn't want to go through that front door, but I knew I had to . . .

When I found myself in the front garden, I felt I had to go in, I just had to. Slowly I tiptoed in, the floorboards screeched! It was then I saw the peculiar shadows. I followed them into all the rooms, then I fell through a trapdoor and there was another door . . .

I walked in. It was the cellar, but my way was now barred. Luckily there was a hole in the wall. I peeped through, I saw my sister. I went to shout her but she walked away. I was trapped in there forever. How was I supposed to get out?

George Cumby (9)
The Latimer School

THE DANGEROUS HOUSE OF DOOM

I stared out of the window and saw the most dilapidated house in the *world!* As I crunched my way up the stony, crooked pathway, I saw dead weeds.

I stepped inside the house and there was dust everywhere. Someone or something flicked something, it felt like water until I noticed it was blood. 'Hello! Anyone there?' I sighed.

As I walked through the house I heard a screeching sound. All of the curtains were tatty, ripped and flapped like a bat's wing. The garden was bare and the treetops were straight. I stifled a scream. I could not walk, I could only limp. I paused for a moment then dust brushed past my face. I looked out of the window and saw the same houses everywhere . . . whatever had happened? I didn't know.

Amber Ward (9)
The Latimer School

THE PROBLEM AT BLACK MANOR

James was going to enter the house of Black Manor. It was dark that night. The trees loomed so high that they looked like peculiar monsters.

Finally he'd reached Black Manor. All he saw was a huge building with three floors and hundreds of stained glass windows. The roof had at least six chimneys. The garden was neglected and nobody had looked after it for years. The grass was long and overgrown with weeds. A spider ran up the garden wall which was rundown.

He rang the doorbell. Aunt Elda opened the door and welcomed him.
'Hello James, I haven't seen you for ages. Come in! I have three hundred rooms. Go up to room fifty please James. That is where you will be staying.'
'Okay Aunt Elda.'

Half an hour later James was in his room unpacking. When he had finished, he changed into his pyjamas and threw himself onto the bed.

An hour later, James woke up and looked around. There was a white shape moving around the room. The shape started wailing, *'Whoooo arrreee youuuuu?'*
James was frozen with fear. He couldn't move a muscle. He screamed and Aunt Elda came and asked him what the matter was.
'There's a ghost in here,' James wailed.

A day later, James was waiting in his bed for the ghost to reappear. When the ghost appeared he introduced himself. 'Hello, I am Ghoulie Ghost. Who are you?'
'I am James. I'm here to make you move house,' James called.
'Well, ha, ha, I won't move,' Ghoulie cackled.

The very next night, James had a plan. Ghoulie came very soon. James was in a monster costume, far scarier than Ghoulie himself. James jumped, Ghoulie screamed.

'Aaaarrgggh! Help!' Ghoulie floated out of the open window and flew off. Ghoulie was never seen again.
James ran downstairs and out of the door.

On the way home, James saw a mirage of Ghoulie. James was safer than mice in a hole.

Rebecca Wilson (8)
The Latimer School

THE LATIMER CASTLE

One night I peered through my window and went out into the night. I woke my three friends, the first was Joe, the second was Bradley, the last was Tom. We all went into my house. Suddenly we heard a scream, we all looked out the window. We saw this thing flashing, so we ran to it and it was a castle. My friend and I went to get a torch, then we all met at the castle. I didn't want to go in but I had to!

When I got into the castle, cobwebs and spiders were everywhere. Ghosts were hiding in secret cupboards and chambers. To get into them, a goblin had a secret key. I ran after him. We came to a river, he took the raft so I took the path. I beat him. He was still going so I caught him. I grabbed the key and chucked him in the river. I ran back to the castle, opened the doors and found ghosts flying everywhere.

I tried to catch them but they were invisible. I put a cloak on. I caught them but one of them dropped out of my hands. I stuffed them back into their places. I tried to catch the boss, but he was too fast. He suddenly bashed into the walls. He was dead so I put him in the river with the goblin.

Kieran McErlean (8)
The Latimer School

LOST AND FOUND

Many years ago in a city far away, the city of Lost and Found, the most scary place became open. A young boy moved in. He went out and he took his dog with him and they happened to walk past a manor. The boy happened to love manors. He knew he had to go in, but the most scary bit about the dilapidated manor was that the doors were wide open. It was dusty and scary.

The boy walked in. Everything was dusty and there was a table in the spooky corner of the manor. On the table were fingerprints. He carried on walking around the manor. There was a door open. He went inside. It was a cellar. He fell down a hole. He found out the manor was a hide. It was a ghost hide and as he fell into the cart, the cart started to move.

An hour later the ride stopped. It had stopped outside an old castle. The boy knew it was a spooky castle, but he loved castles even more than manors. He went into the castle. It was so spooky. He found a hole in the wall and so he climbed through.

There was a petrol station and there was a van. One of the van's doors were open, so the boy jumped in and got home safely.

Thomas Johnson (9)
The Latimer School

THE BEHEADED HOUSE

The oak door swung open. I stepped inside and the door slammed behind me. It was pitch-black. Inside, I gazed around, looking for danger around me. Unbeknown to me a cobweb brushed past my face. My blood ran cold. I stood motionless and I stifled a scream. A sound came from nowhere. The staircase crackled. I tried to get out, but my way was barred. 'Get a grip!' I stammered. I thought it was a dream but it wasn't . . .

Kirsty Bott (9)
The Latimer School

THE HOUSE OF DEATH

I gazed out of the window and saw it. It was the dusty, dilapidated house. In the distance I could see a meandering, raised pathway leading to the house. On one rusty old hinge a door was swinging in the breeze. I looked at the windows, they were smashed and vandalised. Ivy on the wall had started growing. The trees started moving from side to side. Something moved in the darkness. The garden was shabby . . .

Before I knew it I was in front of the door. Suddenly it creaked open. I stepped inside. Something brushed past my face. I made my way forwards. It started to get darker and darker.

It was then I saw something. I just knew someone was there, but I did not know who. I carried on walking until I came to a screeching halt. It was then when I came to a mirror. As I peered into it, something moved behind me. What was I going to do . . . ?

I started to go in every room. The ones that I had been into had traps in, one of the traps got me. It took me somewhere I had never been before. Eyes in the portraits started to move. My heart was pounding, hairs on my neck stood up. I started running everywhere until I got tired. I came to a chair so I could sit down. The door locked so I could not get out.

There was a window in the empty, dusty room. I pulled myself up, my legs just made me go to the window. I peered out across the road, all that I could see was another haunted house . . .

Bradley Hillsdon (8)
The Latimer School

Boo's Revenge!

Kelly and Elle shuddered, teeth chattering, as a cold ripple whistled through the castle spires. A creak came from a wooden rope bridge leading up to the castle. The walls shook. An orange glow reflected against the crumbling cliffs.

'Kelly, where are we? This is all your fault.'
'Why is it my fault? You're the one who brought us here.'
'No I didn't!'
Slowly, still arguing, the voices faded as Elle and Kelly stumbled with fear towards the castle, scared but aware. Kelly's sleek blonde hair and opal eyes twinkled in the darkness. Elle's short auburn hair flicked off the back of her peachy neck.

They slowly started to creep towards the rope bridge. Sparks flew, bubbles emerged from the boiling lava. Grabbing each other's hand they ran along the bridge. An owl hooted and chaos struck as bats flew everywhere.

12 o'clock chimed. As the ground shook they had no choice but to go inside. They grabbed the rusty old door handle in fear! All turned to calm. Nowhere to go but the castle; the door creaked as they opened it, dreading what was inside.
'What, what if . . . ?' Elle said, stuttering.
They hesitated.
'Hurry up, what is it?'
'You know the, erm, ghouls . . . and ghosts,' still stuttering.
They stepped into the castle.

'Footsteps!' they cried, heading towards the door, but they were stopped by something, something strange. They looked up, nothing was there until . . . a cloak was thrown on the floor. It was green velvet. They followed the cloak with their eyes. They peered up and gazed at the amazing sight.
'Hi, I'm Skeli the skeleton and I'm here to help.'
'Help? Help who?'
'You!'

'Do you really mean that?'
'Yes.'
He looked up.
'Boo!'
Skeli trembled.
'Who's Boo?'
'The king of the ghosts.'
Kelly and Elle ran up onto the balcony.
'You can't do this to me, I'm king of the ghosts!'
'Yeah we know!'
With one throw they chucked him over the balcony. They brushed their hands clean, eager to find out how they got there.

All of a sudden they were blinded by a looming light, it was so unbearable they had to turn away. The light faded and uncovered a beautiful mansion, marble floors and more. They blinked unbelievingly at the sight.

Will it last? Will they stay forever? How did they get there?

Cara Stenhouse (10)
The Latimer School

THE BIG PROBLEM

Michelle, Mandy and their aunt Clare moved house on Friday 13th June. After a journey of ten miles they felt really tired. When they had got to the house, they unpacked their cases and found a box filled with blood and they were terrified! They didn't want to look at it anymore so they went straight to bed. Suddenly the door slammed shut! They stayed awake half the night.

Aunt Clare was just sitting outside admiring the house. She was looking through the bathroom window, daydreaming. Suddenly she felt goosebumps over her arms. She saw something move. She ran upstairs and went to bed.

In the morning, Michelle went into the cellar to get her Coco Pops. Suddenly the wine bottles started to shake. All three floated towards her.
'Pick one!' a deep voice boomed. 'Or else.'
Which one, she thought. *I'll pick the mid . . .* she paused, *no, I'll pick the first one.*
'OK, ha, ha - you picked the wrong one!' the voice shouted. 'Grrr!'
Suddenly a gigantic spirit flew out of a bottle. Michelle chucked a book at the spirit and it laughed an evil laugh.
'Ha! Ha! Ha! You'll never hurt me.'
Michelle screamed, 'Help!'
Mandy and Aunt Clare came rushing into the cellar and the two other wine bottles had spirits coming out of them. It seemed as if the whole cellar had been chucked at them. Spirits couldn't die. They fought for ages. Everything had spirits coming out of them. The king spirit just lay back. Then Michelle had an idea, she ran and grabbed the hoover. She switched it on and sucked the spirits down the hoover. They roared with fright and were gone forever.

Aunt Clare rang a demolisher and they demolished the house. Aunt Clare, Michelle and Mandy moved next door and they lived happily ever after.

Charlotte Farmer (8)
The Latimer School

MURDER MANSION

Creak! The old rusty gate swung open, revealing the ancient, desolate mansion. Ivy hung off the balconies and the stone patios were cracked and battered. There were vast grounds surrounding the mansion full of trees and bushes.

'Look at the time, it's 9.35. We'll be late for the party!' exclaimed Matt, a dark haired teenager with wide blue eyes and small ears. His leather jacket blew in the wind as his jeans rubbed together.
'We'll never get there on time!' replied Callum, a green-eyed, small-nosed teen with light ginger hair.
'We'll take a short cut through that mansion, it'll be quicker!' shouted Matt.
'But . . . they call that the Murder Mansion!' answered Callum.
'You don't believe that rubbish do you?' asked Matt sarcastically. 'Come on!'

As they entered the mansion, the giant oak doors slammed shut. As they shut, everything became black like the night sky. Suddenly the torches on the walls lit, revealing the long, dark corridors. There was a strong smell of garlic hanging around. Scott and Callum made their way down the old dusty corridors trying to find the back door.

Suddenly arrows flew out of the walls! Matt heard a thump behind him. He turned and saw Callum on the ground.
'Callummmm!'
He was *dead!*

Matt, still grieving over Callum's death, ran down the corridors! Turning left and right, he came face to face with the back door. He made a run for it!

Suddenly he was falling, falling, falling . . .

Ross Cherry (10)
The Latimer School

THE HAUNTED HOUSE AND THE CURSE OF THE EVIL FLEA

Tom, Ryan and their dog, Tizer, went down to the haunted house because they didn't believe in ghosts. They opened the broken and boarded-up door. They entered in without fear until the door closed automatically. Then there was a voice.

'Who dares enter my lair?' thundered the evil flea.

They tried to find their torches but Tizer wanted his doggy treats and snatched the bag and dragged it through the dog flap in the back door.

Tom was scared, Ryan was nowhere to be seen. The evil flea gave Tom a wedgie and peered into the distance. Tom tried to get out, but the door would not budge. Tom started to panic until Ryan whispered to him.

'Tom, *psst,* over here.'

'Where are you?' said Tom.

'Down here.'

'Hi,' Tom said.

'OK,' mumbled Ryan.

Suddenly the floor lowered down into the flea's lair. They had their eyes shut.

'So you thought you could escape my lair, but you can't. Ha! Ha! Ha! Ha!'

They slowly opened their eyes and a puff of smoke suddenly appeared. It was the evil flea with a rattling gun. He shot at Tom.

Tom woke up. It was all a dream, or was it . . . ?

Liam Green (10)
The Latimer School

THE STRANGE GRAVEYARD

The graveyard looked haunted and spooky. I had gooseflesh all over and was frightened. The gravestones were crumbling, ragged and weird, so I kept looking at them. It was really creepy. Screaming noises and growling were coming from them. I was petrified. Suddenly I saw some wide eyes in the shadows. My toes were trembling, my legs were shivering and I had butterflies in my tummy.

The roof was broken, the garden was battered and the weeds were overgrown.

Suddenly the church shattered even more. The windows smashed, the chimneys were rundown, it seemed creepier. Now my toes were trembling and I had gooseflesh. The roof was battered and the doors were no more. Now it looked really scary. I was really frightened and it looked weird and strange and there was blood all over the walls, the trees were battered and the chairs were destroyed.

A moment later I saw an ugly shadow. It was hideous. I went into the church, the chairs were battered and the walls were pulverised. I thought they'd set traps for me. I saw the shadow again. I thought someone was following me. Suddenly, *crash!* I fell into a hole. Then the shadow appeared. It was the goblin, the ugly goblin.
He said, 'I'm an evil, hideous goblin. Ha! Ha! Ha!' The goblin went for a nap. It was a big nap. He came back with another laugh. 'Ha! Ha! Ha! Ha!' He tripped, he fell down the hole and got knocked out.

I climbed up. He ran after me so I climbed up a tree. 'I've made a plan.' I shot a branch so it fell on him. I killed him and got to school.

Marco Plume (9)
The Latimer School

THE DEADLY CURSE OF THE HOMEWORK

It was 3.15 (the end of school) and Sophie, who had long, shiny brown hair, with glittery eyes and pure red lips, and Lauren, who had sleek brown hair, big blue eyes and pinkish colour lips, were playing hide-and-seek. The hours went by and the clock struck five. The doors closed with a squeak and a band. Sophie and Lauren bolted to the door as fast as they could but . . . they were stuck. They sat down and started to cry. Their heads were down but then suddenly, their heads rose as they heard footsteps. As these people walked closer, they found out it was their enemy, Elle and Naomi . . .

Elle had short blonde hair with sparkly brown eyes and small blue lips and Naomi had a pink bob, dull green eyes and sticky-out lips.
'What you looking at?' chucked Elle with attitude.
'N . . . n . . . nothing,' replied Lauren.
They argued and argued and still argued until it was dark, which was about 9pm. Elle, Sophie and Lauren were asleep, but Naomi stayed wide awake. As the clock struck 12, there was a bang on the door.

As Naomi was lying awake worrying about the bang . . . a crash came from the outside and made her shake with fear. Suddenly, a man came through the door with a gun in his pocket. As he took the gun out of his pocket, he pulled the trigger back. With a scream, a bullet emerged out of the gun and Naomi was dead. As the murderer ran out of the door, a photo fell out of his pocket. Sophie, Lauren and Elle quickly woke up.
'Arghhh!' They all screamed. Luckily, Lauren had her phone with her.
'Quick, quick an ambulance and police. Come straight away,' said Lauren in a hurry.

Elle was crying. The ambulance came, but sadly, Naomi was dead. Then MIT came down as fast as they could, but a clue came to their attention. A photo of Mr Gooding, the deputy head and his family. Then a second clue was found, the deputy head's keys were in the door. Suddenly, Mr Gooding came, looking confused.
'I'm sure I put my keys in my bag, but they're not there, I must have left them at school,' Mr Gooding explained, still looking confused.

'Mr Gooding, I am arresting you on suspicion of murdering Naomi Jade Harrtop,' said one of the MIT girls, with a serious voice.
'OK, I admit that I killed her, but I only did it because she didn't do her homework,' replied Mr Gooding.
'Don't be so stupid!' the MIT said.

Naomi was now a ghost and she flew down to give Mr Gooding her homework, as he was in prison. Would Mr Gooding get out of prison and kill again, or will he have learnt his lesson . . . ?

Sophie Landon (10)
The Latimer School

THE HAUNTED HOUSE

There was a haunted house that was creepy and old. It was on my street. The doors were closing and opening. There were dead flowers everywhere in the garden. The trees looked like they had scary faces, the gates were banging, the birds were screeching in the trees, it was scary.

There was a light on at the top window. There was a face in the window. There, a giant was being chased. He found a door, but he couldn't get in. A fairy came and made the giant little so he could get through the door, but he still couldn't get in as he was much too big and the door was getting smaller and smaller. So was the house.

So the fairy made him even smaller, but as he got smaller the house got bigger so he couldn't reach the handle. The fairy turned him bigger again and then he opened the door and he went in.

The giant looked around, then he heard a snap. It came from upstairs, so he went up. A ghost popped out of a room and scared the giant. He shouted, 'Fairy, come now!' but the fairy did not come, so the giant ran.

Katie-Mae Moran (8)
The Latimer School

DARK WOOD DEATH

Silence echoing . . . gloom thundering . . . over the dusty plains. Humans had departed to escape the zombies!

The female zombie, Veenamis, is a moody, murky, bleak, evil blob. Veenamis has never eaten a Kompanionsivad before, they're live zombie food.

Tonight, Veenamis had different plans. 'Tonight,' she announced, 'I am going to eat . . . a Kompanionsivad! Anyone who objects . . . try to stop me!' muttered Veenamis, through gritted teeth.
'Go! Veenamis! Go!' came the screams from her audience.

So, next day, Veenamis set off on her lingering journey to the creepy Unknown Woods. When finally she reached the woods, with the trees looming high over her head, she peered through the gnarled branches, that seemed to be trying to strangle her!

'We now have new shields to protect us!' the King of Kompanionsivad announced, to the other Kompanionsivads, who were spiky, furry, dwarfish animals, who feared other creatures. 'I . . .' he came to a halt. Sniffed . . . his hideously unattractive face wrinkled at the revolting, pungent smell. Again he sniffed, stepped from the cobwebbed grave he had perched himself on and paced daringly over towards the edge of the clearing. Suddenly, he spotted something; some soul-sucking, gut-spilling, throat-slitting thing . . . Veenamis . . . gasping at the relief of what the elevating shadow was . . . she pounced . . . !

Squirming, screeching, ordering her to let him go; it didn't work! *Slurp!* 'Ewwww!'
'What?' Some people hadn't quite realised yet, what had happened. Their leader had been exterminated.

Veenamis, a broad grin spread across her face, returned swiftly back to her hutch. She was proud of her day's catch. When she got back to her ruins, though a full moon, the wind howling, a scream . . .

Naomi Hartopp (9)
The Latimer School

THE UNDERTAKER

At the graveyard, at midnight, as the thunder bellowed behind the moon, at the undertaker's house, in front of you, Viviene and Mitch dared each other to stop there for a week.

The door was rusty and Viviene screeched! She had never seen the undertaker's house before. Big, lumpy, red blood dripped off the window sill. Curtains were blowing in the wind. They heard a thump. It stopped. *Thump!*

They heard somebody humming the Wedding March. Mitch screeched, they thought a madman was in there. They ran and ran . . . but it stopped. They met back up and turned the doorknob slowly and worriedly.

They heard the Wedding March again, they crept up slowly, slowly, slowly. They ran outside, 'Argghh!' They hid behind the dripping car. There was blood dripping off the car. *Brmm, brmm.* The lights went off and the car furiously moved and crashed into the house. Luckily they weren't in the car, but it was scary and unusual . . .

They went in once again, sat down, the door slammed shut and locked itself. The lights went out and they shouted, 'We've got to get out of here!' but they couldn't, the doorknob fell off . . . they found a candle with blood dripping off it.

Old, ragged, spooky pictures shattered on the floor. It was nothing but the wind and red, salty blood. They cried, 'I miss my mummy!' They sobbed and sobbed and sobbed. Something slowly walked across the floor. They looked, it was too late. They hid behind the blood-covered trapdoor, the person was downstairs . . .

Thump, thump, thump. As they were hiding a voice sweetly said, 'Come out children.' They came out, but nobody was there. They happily ran out.

Joshua Carter (9)
The Latimer School

FLESH EATERS

I was a normal boy until I had a big scare two yers ago on the stroke of midnight. I was walking home from a football match I had had with my friends. I had my remote control car with me and I was walking by the side of the cemetery. I stopped, an old rat ran out with no tail and only one eye, so I ran into the cemetery.

I'd forgotten all about my remote control car that I had left on the graves. Suddenly, I heard a voice, like soil falling from a hill. I turned around and there it was, a giant flesh-eating zombie. I screamed for my life.

The two graves next to the zombie started to move. Suddenly, two more zombies came out. I started to move backwards but tripped over a rock and then I knew I was going to die. In the background, I saw a shadow and when it came into the light, I saw it was my sister. She picked up a cross and shoved it in the zombies' eyes. The zombies slowly crept away into the dark shadowy graves. I knew they'd be back, but not for a very long time.

George Thornley (10)
The Latimer School

HILDA'S BACK

It was the very first night in our new house. There was a raging storm. The banisters, stairs and ceilings were creaking. The next day I rang my best friend, Chelsea and said she could stop the night.

Chelsea came at 4pm. We stayed up so late and then we turned off the light. After ten minutes, Chelsea said, 'Lauren! Turn the light on!'
'Why?' I yawned.
'Well, look over there. Is that Hilda?' Chelsea asked.
'If she has got a purple dress on, got brown hair, is quite podgy, then yes!' I replied.
It was now 4.30am. We both got up and switched the lights on. We watched some TV. Just then we heard a noise.
'What was that?' I whispered.
We went into the dining room and the computer buzzed on.
'What? How . . . ?' Chelsea began.
'Face it Chelsea, it was Hilda.' I explained, looking very worried.
'I'm so, so scared!' sobbed Chelsea.
We told each other jokes and fairy stories to take our minds off *(ahem)* you know who!
'Why did we move here?' I said to myself.

My mum said Chelsea could stay longer if she wanted to. We phoned Chelsea's mum and she could stay longer. It was Chelsea's fourth night here and that night we went to bed quite early. We woke up. It was 2am. 'Oh no!' we cried. The room was full of flames; bright red, orange and yellow!
'How are we gonna get out of here?' I yelled.
Within ten minutes we were crying! We both sobbed. It was 4.30am and guess what? We were at the fire station.
'I am so glad we are out of there!' I said, joyfully.

'Yeah! I didn't think we would get out!' Chelsea replied, relieved.
'Let's go to the house, to see if Hilda is still there,' I said.
We went to the house and entered the front door. It was in ruins! Hilda was gone!

Or was she?

Lauren Akiens (10)
The Latimer School

A MYSTERY

It was a cold night, everybody was asleep except for two little girls. They were called Katie and Mandy. Katie had blonde hair and blue eyes. Mandy had brown hair and brown eyes.

They were walking home from school at 6pm when they came to a haunted house.
'Come on, let's go in,' whispered Katie.
'No, no. It looks too freaky.'
'Chicken! *Cluck, cluck, cluck!*' Katie said, laughing.
'Don't call me that! Come on then, let's go in.' Mandy said, shaking.

'Right, we have been in, now let's go,' said Mandy, walking out.
'Wimp!' Katie said, quietly.
'Let's go upstairs then if you are calling me a wimp,' said Mandy, still shaking.
They got up there when they heard . . . *bang!*
'W . . . w . . . what was that?' said Mandy.
'Sshhh!'
'Oooooo!'
'Alright, show your face,' shouted Katie. It peeped around the corner. 'Come here!' But it turned around and ran as fast as it could. It shot at them and was never seen again.

Lucy Clarke (10)
The Latimer School

IN THE GRAVEYARD

Once upon a time, there lived three brothers called Matt, Scott and Jim. Scott was 15, Matt was 12 and Jim was 10.

One day they were late for school, so they took a shortcut through the graveyard. In the middle of the graveyard there was a house. The garden there was overgrown with weeds and battered flowers. There was a window open, so the boys got closer to the house.

They were eager to go in because they knew a mystery surrounded the house. They stepped inside the haunted house, hearts beating with fear. They heard the door shut and found they were locked in the haunted house.

First they went upstairs and saw a flashing light. They followed it into the master bedroom and there they saw a big dog. The dog chased them downstairs and into the toilet where there was a window in the top, left-hand corner. They smashed it and got out but the dog chased them into the graveyard.

The dog had cornered them and was running towards them and was about to eat them, when the dog jumped up and came at Jim. Jim jumped out of the way and the dog hit the wall. They then managed to run away, as the dog was too hurt to follow them.

Arjun Kanwar (8)
The Latimer School

GONE

Three boys went for the ball which they had kicked over an old mansion's fence. As they approached the dilapidated mansion the front gate, they noticed, was all twisted metal and black paint was flaking off. They pushed it open, it was heavy, and stepped up the path to the doorway. All the pebbles were sticking out of the concrete and Jack tripped over one and sprained his ankle.

As they reached the door, they saw a dog flap, as the door was locked, it was the only way to get in. They didn't want to go in, but they did.

Inside the boys found themselves facing the massive T-shaped staircase. There were moose heads, sharks' teeth, a shotgun and other animal heads hung up on the wall. Aaron said, 'Are you two thinking what I'm thinking?'
They both said, 'Yeah.'
They all whispered, 'Great Grandpa is a hunter.'
All of a sudden, the things on the wall started to move, the shark teeth started chomping and the moose head was swinging from side to side as if it were alive.

They tiptoed up the stairs, avoiding the moving heads. 'C'mon, this way,' demanded Aaron.
They crept off into the first master bedroom. It had a huge bed with paisley covers on it and paisley wallpaper. It was very old-fashioned. There was also a lot of paintings. They went into the second master bedroom and it was exactly the same as the other. They went up another flight of stairs.
'Which room shall we go into?' asked Jack.
'I know,' said John.
'What?' said Aaron.
'Eenie, meenie, minie, mo,' said John.
It was the one in front. They opened the door and found a ghost with an axe. Jack looked behind and said, 'G-g-g-*ghost! Run!*'

They all ran into the front room and locked the door. (They forgot ghosts could go through walls and doors). They were now locked in, but Aaron and Jack climbed out of the window and got away, forgetting about John, who no one heard of again.

Nathan Dale (9)
The Latimer School

MICHELLE'S CHOICE

One dark, gloomy night, Michelle went to the shops and bought some sweets. She was so tired that she went to the most ancient house on the street. She gazed through some rusty, broken windows. The roof was quite cold and dusty and the door handle was twisting madly. The flowers looked like they need a good watering. The gates were about to break down. The garden next door looked so neat, it made the ancient house look disgusting. Michelle was petrified. The bricks were losing their reddish colour. The house number said, 'Creepy Number Eight'. That gave Michelle goosepimples. It was quarter-past twelve and she was so tired her eyelids were about to drop off. As Michelle couldn't see much as she wore glasses, she thought she saw a light on in the dusty, old room. In the corner of the window she noticed lots of cobwebs and was soon frightened. She knew she had to go into Creepy Number Eight!

Michelle opened the door and went in. She found five doors that led into chambers and decided the pick the cleanest of them all, but what she didn't realise, was that it was the scariest of them all. She went through and found bats flying everywhere. Michelle saw cobwebs everywhere. Some the floorboards were missing and her foot was trapped. Michelle saw a door saying *master bedroom*. She went in and saw lots of portraits on the mouldy walls.

Her fingers were trembling as Michelle whispered, 'I want to go home!' Michelle then heard something and swung round so fast, that her glasses came off. All of a sudden she heard a loud *crash*. It was her glasses. Tears came running down her long, droopy face.

She turned round and saw something white. It was a ghost. The ghost had a see-through sword and tried to kill her. She ran down the passageway. Michelle fell and the sword came to a stop. She cried so loudly that the wall shook. Michelle had to use the last of her power to get rid of that white, wicked ghost. She realised she had ghost power and tried to get rid of the ghost, but he held on to Michelle's arm.

Michelle couldn't get the creepy ghost off her arm, while the ghost laughed his head off. Eventually the ghost let go and Michelle was quite proud of herself. Michelle went out of the chamber and went out to the rusty front door. She went through the spooky graveyard and heard a creepy noise. She heard it again and found a dead person on the ground. Michelle held her mouth as she tried to get out of the graveyard, but she couldn't. Then someone said, 'Say the password.' Michelle couldn't think of it at first, but then she said, *'Ghost.'* The rusty gates opened and she went home.

Georgia Groome (8)
The Latimer School

WALKING THROUGH A HORRID HOUSE

One day, Charlie was walking to the shop and saw a house. It had a door that had nearly fallen down and the windows were breaking apart. He was very scared. It looked like the whole house was going to fall down. Charlie knew he had to go in.

As time went by, Charlie said, 'Come on Megan and Jack, we have to go in.'
'But I don't want to,' said Jack.
'Neither do I,' said Megan.
'But we have to!' shouted Charlie, 'We will go in!'

By the time they had stopped arguing it was very late. 'Oh no! I'm going to be late. I'm never going to get home in ten seconds!' So they decided not to go into the haunted house because they would get very told off and sent to bed. As they walked home, Charlie felt frightened again, as he thought someone was following them. Charlie turned around in fright, very nervously but no one was there, so they carried on and finally got home.

Bethany Covill (8)
The Latimer School

THE SCARY STORY

Once, there were two girls, one called Megan and the other called Kate. The two girls went out at 10 o'clock every night. One night they came to a house. It looked haunted and was battered. The gate was crooked and rusty. My name is Hollie and I was with them that night.

I squeezed through the gate and walked up to the house. My friends followed behind.

As we went in the house, Megan saw a witch. The witch cast a spell on me and then vanished. She later appeared where Kate was. Kate tried to scream, but she couldn't. Megan came running out shouting, 'Kate! Kate! Where are you?' There was no answer. Megan looked round the corner and Kate was there, frozen with fear.

We woke her up and ran home. The witch vanished and was never seen again.

Hollie Preston (9)
The Latimer School

THE SECRET GAME

Ben and Josh were playing catch outside the haunted mansion on Friday night. The windows were smashed and the door handle was rusty. There were tattered curtains and the drainpipe was hanging off. They carried on playing catch. Josh chucked the ball and it landed in the haunted mansion. They did not want to go into the rundown, haunted mansion, it looked too spooky and haunted but Ben wanted to go in. There was ivy grown up the wall and they knew they had to go in to get the ball and their dog, who had also ran in.

Ben and Josh walked in. From the inside it looked spooky and the walls were crumbling. In the middle of the room there was a set of stairs. At the top of them there was a stool. On the stool was a box. Ben and Josh walked up to the box, surrounded with plants. Inside was a game.

A moment later they heard a voice, 'Get away from the game. It's bad, don't open it.' They looked around and saw something coming out of the wall. It was a little ghost, followed by nine others, all shouting, 'Don't open the game. It's bad!'

The ghosts flew after Ben and Josh and somehow the game opened and sucked all of them in! They were now inside the game, but could they finish it? Ben said, 'It's a maze.'
'But we might never leave,' Josh said.
Ben though that the ghosts might have played the game and got lost. 'We might never escape and become ghosts like them,' he said aloud. 'Look,' said Ben, 'a sign. It says *find the keys to unlock the doors.*' Ben found an open door with a table in the room behind. On the table was a key. There was also a sign on the key which said, *find the door with a sword on it.*

They found the door with the sword on it and it opened. There was their dog, with the ball in his mouth. They found the exit and went home.

They did not want to go back to the house ever again.

Alexander Morrison (9)
The Latimer School

SPOOKY STORY

The house had been forbidden for 1 million years. I was trembling. I was petrified as I peered through the window. I walked round to the back garden and there was a hole in the grass, the brickwork was crumbling down. I had wide eyes and was frozen with fear.

Alice was going upstairs to bed. She got ready and went to bed.

In the morning Alice got dressed and went downstairs for breakfast. After breakfast, she watched TV. Then she went back upstairs and found a secret door through the stairs.

Jack and Bill followed behind Alice as she hurried down and found a way to a secret cave.

They ended up in the garden where they had found a hole in the ground. Alice, Jack and Bill walked up to the hole and out came a giant ant. It had laser eyes and shot at them, but Alice and her friends managed to dodge it. A magic sword popped into Jack's pocket, so Jack stabbed the giant ant and was never to be seen again.

Jared Pickering (9)
The Latimer School

PETRIFIED POWER

On a cold summer's night, there was a crash of thunder and a loud screaming noise. Skater Boi stood up in bed in shock. 'W-what's that? W-where's it coming from?' He tried to ignore it but he couldn't get to sleep.

The next day was sunny, so Skater Boi decided to go out on his skateboard and call for JJ. 'Hello? Anyone there?' No one answered at JJ's house, so Skater Boi went back to his house.

A few hours later Skater Boi called for JJ again. There was a voice coming from Skate Boi's mum.
'And where do you think you're going?'
'Erm . . . erm . . . round JJ's house.'
'And what were you going to do there?'
'Nothing,' he exclaimed.
'Well come back this instance.'
'Oh do I have to?'
'Go to your room.'
Skater Boi didn't mind going to his room because he could climb out of his window.

He called for JJ again. His mum answered the door. 'Hi, is JJ there?'
'Yes, he is, I'll get him for you Skater Boi.'
I heard the screaming noise but louder.
'Hi,' said JJ in a squeaky voice, 'I've lost my voice.'
'Well can you play out?'
'Yeah!'

They played on the half pipe until dark and then they ran back home, but they found themselves lost. They next saw a dark, gloomy shed. Skater Boi opened the door and a big white thing popped out screaming!
'That screaming is familiar! It's that screaming I heard before!' said Skater Boi.
They ran back home as fast as they could, but just then Skater Boi noticed that he had forgotten his skateboard.

The next day, Skater Boi called for JJ.

'Hi, do you want to go to the *creepy* shed again, cos I've lost my board.'

'Pardon?'

'Do - you - want - to - go - to - that - creepy - shed?'

'OK! I heard you the first time!'

They walked very slowly. Skater Boi heard the screaming noise again. Skater Boi ran off and left JJ on his own.

The next morning Skater Boi went back to the shed. He found JJ, petrified. He sprinted into the shed.

'Ha! Ha! I'm going to do the same as I did to your friend. Petrify you!' said the ghost.

Why is it always me? thought Skater Boi.

Adrienne Coulter (10)
The Latimer School

GOLDEN ALONE SCHOOL

Creak, creak, the door swished open and the four friends were amazed at Golden Alone School. They crept up the twelve steps.

'I hated this school,' muttered Tanya.

Michelle pushed the door open. Ashley, Michelle, Neco and Tanya were standing in the boys' abandoned cloakroom. Neco saw his PE bag and took it off the peg. He looked inside it and it smelt like disgusting cheesy feet.

'You won't be needing that thing on the way!'

They all walked on into Mrs Fiddle's old classroom. She was annoying, she always fiddled. No wonder she was called Mrs Fiddle. They all laughed except for Michelle, who asked, 'What's so funny?'

'I learned from that times tables chart,' chuckled Ashley.

They all turned and looked around and then stared at the times tables chart but it wasn't a times tables chart any more it was spellings.

'Is it me, or was that times tables before?' whimpered Tanya.

'Come on, let's get out of here!' squawked Ashley.

They all went out and Michelle was the last one out. The door was locked and it wasn't locked before. They all looked like their eyes were going to pop out and then they screamed.

'Something is very dodgy. I mean first the times tables and then the door. Something's very fishy,' whispered Tanya.

'Come on let's go into Mrs Rushin's class. She was nice. Even though she'll be a ghost, she'll be a nice ghost,' smiled Neco.

'Come on then,' smiled Michelle as they went in. 'Ah it's just the same,' she said.

'Oh my goodness, it's Mrs Rushin as a ghost,' said Tanya.

'Hello,' said the ghost. 'It's my four favourite pupils,' and she smiled at them.

'Come on you guys, she's freaking me out,' muttered Tanya.

'What the . . .'

All of a sudden Mrs Rushin chopped Ashley's head off and disappeared.

'Come on. If you're not coming, I'm still going,' sobbed Tanya.

'Yes we should go,' the rest retorted.

Michelle, Neco and Tanya went through the corridors and came to a halt. There were booming noises. 'Come on don't stop!' they all shouted and they ran down the twelve steps.

Step by step, they went and they all escaped.

Charlotte Harrison (9)
The Latimer School

SKULL DEATH

As the clock struck for 12 midnight. A bang boomed down the street past Scott's and Santos' ears. Something white appeared in the road. What was it?

Santos is 15, he loves cricket but plays football. He is a teenager with attitude and has a nickname. His mum's from India but sadly his dad died from SARs.

As for Scott he is a year older than Santos. His mum and dad are still alive, so Scott teases Santos a lot. Scott has no nickname, although Santos likes to call him 'Scotty Boy'. Scott doesn't like that of course.

'W-What's that?' said Santos.
'What?' said Scott.
'It's a skull,' stuttered Santos.
'Is not.'
'Is too.'
'Is not.'
'Is too.'
'What is it then?'
'A bone, Durr.'
'. . . A skull is a bone you dipstick.'
'Ow!'
'Thank you.'
'Stop being a know-it-all,' shouted Scott.

They edged closer to the skull. They felt a shiver run down their spines. Suddenly another bang roared down the street.
'Roar!'
'Who said that?' shivered Scott
'I don't know,' said Santos quietly.
Just then a flash appeared by a tree. The flash was followed by another flash and another and then three owls fell out of the tree.

The next day shadows kept appearing and later that night Scott was woken by a scream. *'Aaarrggh!'*

The next day a Zombie appeared. A roll of thunder roared and a ball of blue floated in the air and hit Santos!

What a weird time!

Daniel Johnson (10)
The Latimer School

THE SPOOKY GRAVEYARD

Introduction
It was a dark, gloomy night in Rainbowland and Sprite was walking home to his house. He forgot the way to his house so he had to take the short cut through the graveyard. It was dilapidated in the graveyard and all the stones were mouldy and broken, cracked and battered. The gate was painted black once, but now all you could see was a rusty metal gate. The church was like a spooky house. Its bricks were falling out and the cement was coming off the bricks.

It was definitely a spooky graveyard.

***

Sprite was sleeping round his friend's house and forgot his clothes, so he said to his friend, 'I'll be back in a jiffy . . . I'm just going to get my stuff.'
'OK then,' said his friend loudly.

Sprite put on his coat and shoes and set off. On the way he forgot how to get home so he had to take the way through the graveyard because by now he was at least a mile away from his friend's house. So it would take nearly two hours to even get near his house. He had to take the short cut through the graveyard. He quietly tiptoed into the spooky graveyard.

Sprite opened the gate, horrified that a vampire would catch him so he walked quickly and quietly. Suddenly a vampire shot up from the ground it was Sir Ulrich Von Lichtenstein, the greatest vampire of all. He walked up to Sprite. Sprite became very scared and gave a deep, deep sigh. The vampire uncovered his sharp white fangs. Sprite was now so scared that he instantly ran as fast as he could but the vampire caught up with him.

'Sir Ulrich Von Lichtenstein is my name. Please tell me yours before I drink your blood!'
Sprite took a deep breath and spoke his name out with the little voice he had left.

Eventually Sprite got out of the graveyard. He was out of breath and ran as fast as he could. When he reached his house he ran to his mum. 'Mum, Mum, help!'

'Sprite, what is it?' said his mum.

'I was nearly killed by a vampire.'

'OK, OK, stay here for the night instead of sleeping round your friend's house. I will call them.'

'OK Mum,' said Sprite in a quiet voice.

'Get ready for bed now then.'

'OK Mum. I love you!'

'I love you too!'

Charley-Ann Freeman (8)
The Latimer School

BEWARE OF THE GHOST

The timber door screeched open, and I peered into the dark, dilapidated house. I stepped forwards onto a creaky floorboard. I could hear a noise, it was coming from a door.

I went to the great hall. A ghost came from behind me. I tried to scream but I couldn't. I stood motionless as the ghost came towards me. I then moved towards a door and let myself in. Something flew at me and there were lots of bats. On the floor I saw lots of daisies. Suddenly the door opened, it was a trap and I fell in it and had to get back into the house. I managed to climb out of the trap.

Then I went home and told my mum about it and she told me that she didn't believe me.

Bethany Varnham Fisher (8)
The Latimer School

THE LATIMER NIGHTMARE

One stormy night five friends were walking down a street when they heard a noise.

'W-w-w-hat was that noise?' whispered Mia.

'I don't know,' yelled Nathan.

'Lets go and see,' replied Neco.

'You must be crazy!' cried Mia.

'No, no, no, we went to this school,' explained Neco.

'B-b-but it might be haunted now,' cried Mia.

'Where did you get that idea from?' mumbled Nathan.

'Well you never know,' replied Mia.

'Never mind. Let's go in,' shouted Neco.

'Do I have to?' sighed Mia.

'Yes, you do!' replied Nathan.

'Well if I have to I will,' sighed Mia being sarcastic.

'Come on then,' replied Nathan. So they all went in.

Nathan fell into a hole.

'Nathan!' yelled Mia.

'Quick get some help!' cried Neco.

'No I don't want to leave him,' cried Mia.

The next day Nathan found himself in hospital on a life support machine. Suddenly Nathan woke up. 'What am I doing here?' he screamed.

'Can't you remember that we all went to the old school and you fell down a hole, as soon as you walked in? explained Mia and Neco.

'But why am I on a life support machine?' asked Nathan.

'Well you're going to die because something got stuck in your heart and they can't get it out,' explained Neco.

'I'm sorry, we will all miss you,' cried Mia.

Hannah Schofield (9)
The Latimer School

A MYSTERY STORY

Emily had long brown hair.
Lucy came out.
'What are you doing?' asked Lucy.
'I don't know,' replied Emily.
'It's boring!' replied Lucy.
'I agree,' muttered Emily.
Emily was very small.
'Come on!' shouted Emily.
'OK,' mumbled Lucy.
They went to the table.
'What are we having for dinner?' asked Lucy.
'Salad for dinner,' replied Emily.

After dinner they went back outside to play.
'What do you want to do?' asked Emily.
'Do you want to come into my bedroom?' asked Lucy.
'OK,' said Emily.
'Can you put the music on please?' muttered Lucy.
'Yes, of course.'

Nearly time for bed
'11 o'clock, bed time,' said Emily.
'Let's go to my bedroom,' said Emily.
They went to bed an hour later.

Emily woke up and she asked Lucy, 'What's that noise?'
'I do not know,' replied Lucy.
'Let's go outside and see what it is,' muttered Emily.
'OK,' replied Lucy.
'Can't see anything,' shouted Emily.
'Lets go back to bed,' replied Lucy.

What was it downstairs . . . ?

Katie Worth (10)
The Latimer School

THE GREAT HOUSES OF DOOM

I peered out of my window and saw a dilapidated house with dead flowers. There were bricks falling from the house.

The timber door screeched open and I peered into the dark house. I stepped forward onto a creaky floorboard. I carried on walking.

I came to a room, a dark room. As I went into the room the front door slammed shut and locked all by itself. I ran and run until I found myself in the great hall. Something in the darkness ran across the hall.

I went looking for it and found a dead end. Something ran away from me. I saw a secret passageway leading out of the house.

I woke up and thought it was just a dream. I looked out of the window and realised then that it wasn't!

Jesse Petty-Gilbert (8)
The Latimer School

HILDA'S REVENGE

There lived an old woman with grey, dirty, scraggy hair. She lived on her own in a spooky castle on a creepy lane.

'Come on Lauren, let's go and explore that castle,' Chelsea said excitedly.
'Go on then!' Lauren whispered in a scared voice.

As they opened the door and looked around the room the door slammed, *bang!* They mturned around slowly.

'Wh-wh-what was that?' said Chelsea feeling scared.
'It must be that ghost I'm always talking about,' explained Lauren.
'You always talk about that ghost, now give it a rest OK!' Chelsea said she was annoyed.
'You will soon find out,' replied Lauren.
'Shut up now!' Chelsea yelled. Her voice echoed around the room and they both looked at each other. 'How's about we leave?' she said.
'That's a good idea,' replied Lauren.

They ran to the door but as they touched the handle, the door wouldn't open. They both shivered for a second.
'Shall we go and explore then,' asked Chelsea.
'Yes,' Lauren said excitedly.

As they explored the house they started hearing noises.
'Chelsea can you hear that?' said Lauren.
'No,' replied Chelsea.
'Must be me,' gulped Lauren and she looked around the room. She could hear the noises but could not see anything.

As they went up the stairs Chelsea was at the back and Lauren was at the front. Chelsea heard a noise behind her. 'Wh-wh-what was that!'
'I don't know,' replied Lauren. But she whispered to herself, 'Hilda!' as a gust of wind swept by her.

They ran down the stairs and to their relief the door was now open. With sighs of relief they ran out and closed the door.

When they reached home they opened the door and tea was on the table and much later that night as they got into bed Lauren said, 'We never got to explore that house did we?'

No, thought Chelsea to herself.

Chelsea Quittenton (9)
The Latimer School

DEAD BODIES

One night there was a spooky road and at the end of that spooky road there was an ancient Victorian house.

'Come on we must go down that road,' whispered Joshua.
'B-but . . . ' stuttered Charlotte, 'I-I . . . ' stuttered Charlotte again.
'Oh spit it out,' shouted Joshua.
'I don't want to die,' cried Charlotte.
'You won't die with me around,' said Joshua with determination.
'How can you be so sure, Josh?' asked Charlotte.
In reply Joshua said, 'Do you want the honest answer?'
'Yes I do,' shouted Charlotte.
'OK, OK, well I don't know,' whispered Joshua.
'What do you mean you don't know?' thundered Charlotte.
'Shhh, keep it down,' said Joshua crossly.

Just then they both heard a bang! (A very big bang indeed).
'What was that?' cried Charlotte and Joshua.
'I'm sure it's nothing,' said Joshua.
'I'm not scared,' said Charlotte in an unconvincing way.
'Then why do you sound scared?' said Joshua.

They both walked down the spooky old road. Just then a scream rang out, *'Argh!.'*
Charlotte and Joshua saw . . . a ghost and a dead body below.

The body looked familiar to Joshua.
'I know who that is, it's my cousin,' cried Joshua.
'Come on, let's go to school,' whispered Charlotte as they walked down the road.
'It's too scary.' cried Charlotte.
'Well it's going to be isn't it?' yelled Joshua.
'I don't like it,' whispered Charlotte.
'I don't either but there you go,' said Joshua sarcastically.

When they got to school the whole class was dead and only Charlotte and Joshua remained alive.

Just then they both heard a big bang and the last thing they remember is knives shooting out of the walls and then they died in a lot of pain . . . but who did it?

Shannen Dowsing (9)
The Latimer School

FRIGHTENING FACTORY

I was walking down the cobbled path with my size three feet crushing the little cobbles, as I stepped one foot after another. Finally I made it to the dilapidated factory. When I looked up at the wall ivy was covering the whole building and there were bricks that had fallen out.

When I climbed through the smashed window, I saw that inside there were all electrical wires stuck to the walls. I walked a little further in.
'Boo!' bellowed Moly.
'*Aaarrgghh,*' cried Chuck. 'Moly you're about to give me a heart attack.'
'Ah, ah, ah,' laughed Moly.
'Come on let's go in,' muttered Chuck.

They walked in and they found some stairs, which only went halfway and there was then a hole right in the middle. They climbed up the stairs and they heard a crack!
'What was that noise!' boomed Chuck.
'I don't know,' cried Moly.
'The st-st-st . . .' Chuck stuttered for a moment.
'What's wrong?' mumbled Moly.
'The stairs are falling,' mumbled Chuck.

They fell through and they shouted as they fell. They then landed with a thud.
'Ouch!' yelled Chuck.
'Ouch!' yelled Moly.
'Where are we?' said Chuck and he sounded very scared.
'I don't know but it's pitch-black and freaky!' replied Moly.
'*Ooohh!*'
'What the hell!' thundered Chuck.

But what was the noise . . . ?

Jack Hall (10)
The Latimer School

THE SCARY STORY

One dark gloomy night Dill saw a haunted house. It looked like it hadn't been looked after for years. Dill thought she should go in and she did. She heard someone calling from the kitchen. She got *sooo* scared. The kitchen looked dilapidated and the paint was flaking off. Dill looked at the dusty stairs, there were cobwebs everywhere. Someone was coming, Dill hid behind the door. It was a model, it looked like a ghost. It was a ghost! But Dill knew she had to go in.

A minute later . . .

Dill heard something. It looked spooky. The floor was creaking as she walked along. The eyes of the portrait looked as if they were following her too. She thought someone was following her and turned around but no one was there. It was dark. One of the portraits fell down which made Dill jump. Someone was behind and it was a witch! She gasped and ran down to the cellar where there were cobwebs everywhere.

A minute later . . .

Dill thought she should get out. She tried all fifteen windows but they were locked. Suddenly she saw one more window, it was worth a try so she went over to it.

It was open and Dill got out the window while the witch tripped over the rope.

Alice Holroyd (8)
The Latimer School

UNTITLED

Once in Portugal there were two boys, who loved playing football. They were called Robbie and William and they both wanted to become professional football players.

They lived near a beach and they went there every weekend but this weekend was not going to be like a normal weekend.

William saw his house, it was a little cottage with a black tiled roof and the walls were made of stone. William went into the house and his mum was cooking tea. William asked, 'Can I go to the beach with Robbie?' 'No,' shouted his mum because she had burnt tea.

When he was crunching on his burnt tea he asked could he go tomorrow so they could explore all day long.

When he was asleep all he could dream of was exploring in the dim, dark caves and seeing what he could find in the rock pools.

The next day William woke up at seven o'clock and quietly said, 'Can I go to the beach with Robbie?' 'Yes,' said his mum still half asleep.

Robbie and William went to the other side of the beach and they went in the biggest cave they'd been in so far, but there was nothing in there. They went in quite a small cave and there was a bottle. William opened it and was just about to drink it when Robbie said, 'No, you don't know what's in there,' but William drank it anyway.

He disappeared. He had turned invisible as well as William. Invisible they were at last.

Robbie got home but William didn't, he went into a sweet shop and ate lots of sweets. After that he read comics in the comic shop.

When he went into the third sweet shop, the drink had worn off and he was stuck in there all night. In the morning the shopkeeper let him out and William said, 'Thank you.' He ran home and hugged his mum and played with Robbie all day long.

Elliot Bastos (9)
Trefonen School

NUTKIN AND THE SQUIRREL FROM THE MOON

One day Nutkin the squirrel was collecting nuts for his breakfast. After breakfast he decided to go and visit his friend, Tiberears the bear. As he was walking to Tiberears' cave he saw a spider stuck in a glass jar.

As Nutkin was a very kind squirrel, he went over to help the spider, but in the process he managed to set the spider free and get himself stuck. Nutkin pushed and shoved, shouted and screamed and even banged the jar on some rocks, but the jar just wouldn't budge! In the end Nutkin gave up and walked the rest of the way to the cave with the jar on top of his head.

When Nutkin got to the cave he shouted Tiberears' name, but as he was in the jar Tiberears didn't hear him. (Anyway Tiberears was snoring loudly.) Eventually Tiberears woke up and saw Nutkin stuck in the jar, but Tiberears thought he was a squirrel from the moon with a spacesuit on.

Clumps the cat came in and pushed the jar over. (They called him Clumps because he was really clumsy.) Tiberears told Clumps about the squirrel from the moon and they started looking for him, and as far as I know they still are.

Siobhan Harvey (8)
Trefonen School

A MESSAGE IN A BOTTLE

It was 1856, on the last day of spring, when Captain Long John Laser Legs was happily cruising on the Red Sea. Laser Legs wasn't a very good captain, for one, he was ugly, and two, he ordered his crew to do things he could do himself.

Suddenly a huge wave sent a tiny bottle flying onto the ship. Captain Laser Legs opened the bottle. Inside was a treasure chart they'd been searching for, for years.
'Wow!' said the crew (who were not all that bad) when they found out. As soon as Laser Legs knew they knew about the chart he ordered them to set sail for Windfall Island.

At last they reached the gigantic island. They anchored the ship and walked up the hot sands to where the treasure was. Alas a huge dragon was guarding the treasure chest. Captain Laser Legs' crew scampered back to the ship as soon as they saw the massive creature. But their brave captain stayed where he was. He was determined to get the treasure. The dragon charged at the captain but he was too quick on his feet. He pulled out his sword and did an almighty throw. The sword landed in the dragon's chest. It roared and rolled over. It was dead.

As soon as he got back to the ship he saw his crew's sympathetic looks, so he shared the treasure with them and they never stole again.

Lucy Meyer (8)
Trefonen School

ELLIOT GETS LOST

Once there lived a 10-year-old boy in Glasgow. His name was Elliot. Both of his brothers were always making lies up about him and his mum was shouting at him. Elliot got fed up and he decided to run away. He packed all the things he needed and climbed out of his window. As soon as he got on his window sill he jumped down and climbed over the wall in his back garden.

After 10 minutes Elliot's oldest brother told another lie. The lie was about throwing stones at his bedroom window. Elliot's mum went into Elliot's bedroom stamping her feet and shouting, 'Elliot, have you been throwing stones?' Suddenly she stopped when she got into his room. She went downstairs, back into the kitchen wondering where Elliot was. Elliot was in the city centre looking at the toys when he felt a pair of cold hands on his arms.

The cold pair of hands frightened Elliot. Then he got picked up. Elliot was struggling and he was trying to say help but it was no good. His grandad saw him and he came racing out of his shop yelling, 'Let go of him!'

A security guard heard all of the shouting and screaming. He turned around on his heel and got the kidnapper. Elliot's gran took him home in her Ford while his grandad went to hospital. Elliot's mum gave Elliot a great big hug. His mum said, 'I'll never shout at you again.' They lived happily ever after.

Greg Stokes (8)
Trefonen School

MESSAGE IN A BOTTLE

One sunny day a girl called Amber and a boy called Sam went to the woods. When they got there they saw a message in a bottle. It was floating in a stream. Sam ran to get it, he pulled and pulled, *pop!* It was out. They both stared at it, it was a treasure map.

A mean boy called Spud snatched it off them. They were extremely sad because they were lost. *Smash!* They turned and right there was smashed glass. Spud was nowhere to be seen.

By the glass there was the message, they both followed the map. A minute later . . . 'Look Sam an X. I wish I had a spade.'
'Let's dig with our hands.'

They dug and dug and they got to the bottom of the hole where they saw a penny, then more pennies. They followed them and got the treasure.

Tom Gale (7)
Trefonen School

SHAURN AND OSCAR

Once, long ago, there was a young girl called Shaurn. She had black hair and she lived in a little cottage near a forest in England. Her dad was named John and he was very friendly. He had gone on holiday a couple of years before.

One sunny Friday morning Shaurn asked her mother if she could have a pet.
'No!' shouted her mother.
Shaurn ran outside into the forest, she had wanted a pet all her life, she was so upset. Then right in front of her was a little kitten. 'Now I've got a pet. I've got a pet!' she exclaimed.

She ran home with a smile on her face. 'Mum, Mum can I keep this kitten please?' she asked. She asked her all morning and afternoon and was so persuasive she just had to say yes. The kitten was black with a white bib.

They looked after Oscar day after day. Then, one blustery Wednesday, Shaurn's mother noticed her daughter had caught a disease. She had caught it from Oscar. She had to stay in bed until she got better.

It was a Sunday night when she recovered from her disease. Oscar had as well. Soon the kitten wasn't a kitten but a cat. Shaurn and Oscar were best friends, her mother was much nicer now.

They went for a walk in the forest and bought their swimming costume and towels and had a swim in the river that flows through it. They went home and there in the doorway was John. They ran to each other and gave each other a big hug (even Oscar).

Liath Campbell (8)
Trefonen School

THE LIVING SNOWMAN

It was the middle of winter and George hated winter, but today it was all different. George was persuading like mad to go outside and play in the snow. George lived in a very old cottage. After a while George got to go outside and play. George wanted to make a snowman so he did. He got two jelly beans for the eyes and a stripy scarf for buttons, a banana for its mouth and a carrot for its nose.

That night when George was sleeping the snowman came to life. The next day George woke up nice and early to see if the snowman was still there. He was amazed it was talking but there was something missing, it's nose. The snowman said, 'A deer took my nose up to the creepy cave where the monster lives!'

That night George got out of bed and climbed up the mountain into the cave, but the monster captured him and he was never seen again.

Jools Phillips (8)
Trefonen School

POTION IN A BOTTLE

One sunny day in Los Angeles there was a girl called Hannah who was quite pretty. She lived with her family in a big old house. That afternoon she decided to go to the beach (by her house) to have a little paddle. She asked her mum, 'Please may I go to the beach, oh please?' 'OK,' said her mother (who was doing the ironing).

Hannah packed a few things and then set off. But when she was playing she saw something in the water. She went a little bit closer hoping it wouldn't be a jellyfish or something. She quickly put her hand in the water. *Splash!* Everyone looked at her, Hannah was quite embarrassed and her face was red.

She looked at the bottle, it read something magic. *Oooo*, thought Hannah, *I shall drink some of this*.

Straight away she was magic. She had a lovely day doing magic. Two hours later everything went wrong because when she made the dog talk, it spoke ancient Egyptian and nobody could understand her. It was terrible, so she went to the beach quite sad.

Hannah found another bottle. That one read, stopping magic. She drank it straight away and she wasn't magic any more.

Alice Roberts (8)
Trefonen School

THE PUZZLE IN THE BOTTLE

'Mum, Mum can we go the beach?'

'If you have brushed your teeth and hair.'

'Yes I have,' shouted Tilly excitedly.

Tilly was ten years old and always helped her mum around the house so she was allowed to have quite a lot of treats.

They packed their bags full of food for a picnic. When they had packed they set off to the beach. They walked the long two miles and at last, they got there. Tilly's mum set out her picnic on the beach.

In a while Tilly got in her swimming costume and paddled in the sea. Suddenly there was a big bang! 'Ow!' shouted Tilly. A glass bottle had hit her foot hard.

Tilly picked up the bottle, there was something inside. She looked around to see if anybody was looking, no one was so she opened it up. There was a map inside.

Tilly told her mum she was going for a walk, then she followed the map. The map led to a tree. Tilly was confused, *a tree,* she thought, she looked at the map again, it was right. Tilly pulled a branch on the tree to see if it was secure to climb.

Suddenly some bark came off the tree and a head popped out. It was a black and white animal. It was a little puppy who was very weak and had got stuck in the tree, he hadn't had food for days. Tilly had bought her backpack with her picnic. She gave the puppy some food, then put him in one of her pockets in her bag. She didn't tell her mum for days but her mum did find out because the fridge door was left open and food was all over the floor and of course there was poo all around the garden.

One night Mum asked Tilly if there was anything wrong because Tilly was acting weirdly lately. Tilly told her and Mum let her keep the puppy.

Emily Morris (9)
Trefonen School

CHLOE'S NIGHTMARE

'Chloe,' shouted her mum.

Chloe was in her bedroom putting make-up on which she wasn't meant to be doing and brushing her long black hair but not tying it up.

'Time for school,' shouted her mum again.

Chloe ran downstairs for breakfast. Her mum obviously sent Chloe back upstairs to wipe her face. But she didn't, she just ran out of the kitchen and out of the front door, slamming it behind her.

Chloe started to walk to school, she had snuck all her make-up in her bag. On the way she saw a girl and teased her because she wasn't as pretty as her. Then she saw a boy and took his lollipop off him. She saw two little girls and pushed them over. Finally she was at school on the playground with her friends, skipping and singing a mean song to the little ones.

When they went in the classroom her teacher was going on and on about how people had to practise their spellings for Wednesday while Chloe was telling her friends about her midnight feast.

'Chloe,' shouted Miss Drury, 'tell me what I said.'

'Um, um don't know Miss Drury.'

All her friends laughed.

'You can stay in at dinner time for 5 minutes.'

When she was allowed out she started playing tig with her friends.

'You can do this and you can do that.'

Suddenly one of her friends stood up to Chloe, 'Stop being so mean to that girl and so bossy to us. We aren't your friends anymore,' said her friends.

'So!' shouted Chloe, 'you're not coming to my midnight feast.'

Her friends, or not her friends ran off including her best one.

Chloe was a laughing stock because she'd started crying. Her friends started to feel sorry for her so they said, 'OK we'll be your friends as long as . . .'
'OK I know.'

Rachael Dowle (8)
Trefonen School

THE TROUBLE WITH JADE

Hi, I'm Jade. Let me tell you a bit about myself. I'm quite tall, I've got long black hair and I'm rather pretty (even though I do say so myself). In fact about the only thing wrong with me is I'm incredibly clumsy, well I was. Should I tell you what happened last week which completely changed my life forever? OK. It all started when I was just about to take my dog for a walk. 'Jade,' my mum called, 'will you go to the market and buy some fruit?' so I ended up taking my dog for a walk.

I looked at the list and it said, oranges, pears, plums, apples and bananas. I wandered over to the plums, but unfortunately someone had left a skateboard lying around and I didn't look where I was going and *splat!* I hate to think about it.

To make matters worse a few kids from school started up a chant, 'Jade fell in the mud, Jade fell in the mud.' I couldn't bear it any longer. I ran and ran and didn't stop running until I reached home. As soon as I got inside my mum started shouting, 'What happened to you, mucky pup?' So I spilled out everything. After I'd explained my mum said, 'Go and run yourself a bath and for goodness sake try not to let it overflow.' Although my mum warned me I forgot, again.

'Jade,' Mum called up, 'what's that awful racket? Argh.' From that scream I could tell something had happened. At first I wondered what could have caused the scream, then it clicked. The bath! Quickly I dashed to the bathroom and turned off the tap.

Later, after I'd cleared up the mess Mum said she was going for a walk. But little did I know she was going to ask all the villagers to send letters to me saying, 'cure your clumsiness'.

In the morning, when I opened all the letters, these letters stuck in my head and I now remember to look where I'm going all the time.

Elise Meyer (8)
Trefonen School

A FRIENDSHIP

One nice sunny day on Beachcomber Bay in the sea there was a dolphin called Flipper and a fish called Eddy. Last of all a shark called Snappy. Snappy wasn't called Snappy for nothing because he was always being greedy and nasty. He was grey on his body at the top, underneath it was white, because he was a great white. Flipper was bluish-grey, he was nice and friendly to people. Last of all the fish called Eddy, he was green as can be, he was nice and friendly as well as Flipper.

Anyway Flipper and Eddy wanted to go somewhere because it was always dull in the same spot, so they decided to go on a little adventure to create the new day. But they had a bit of trouble coming their way because Snappy was coming after them because he wanted to get something to eat as he hadn't had any breakfast yet, and wanted Flipper and Eddy for his breakfast.

They swam like the waves but Snappy was the fastest swimmer in the sea when there's food about of course. But first Snappy chased Eddy and he nearly got caught, but Flipper headbutted Snappy and got kicked out and Eddy was a bit hurt because Snappy bit him just a little bit and he was bleeding a little. They cleaned him up.

After that they were off to go and find somewhere else. Then they went too far because they were right at the shore and a huge wave pushed them on to the shore. They tried to get off but they couldn't. In an hour they'd finally got off.

A strange thing was on the shore, it was round and it was a ball, but they didn't know that it was a ball because they'd never seen a ball before. A child then told them what it was. They kept the ball and went home but will Snappy think of a plan to get the ball?

Zoe Matthews (8)
Trefonen School

THE OLD SHED

In a funny land there lived a girl called Reaner. She lived on a big farm, there were chickens, horses, pigs, cows, geese, dogs, a cat and sheep. Reaner had to look after the farm because her mum was not well.

One day she went to count the chickens, one was missing. She looked everywhere, behind the barn, in the barn, behind the hay, in the garden, down the road, but she could not find the missing chicken.

Suddenly she heard the hen and she saw the hen, it ran into the shed. Reaner had never seen this shed, so she walked slowly to it.

She found the hen and she picked her up and came back later.

When she got in the shed she saw something sparkling, it was a diamond necklace and it was magic. She grabbed the necklace and took it and hid it.

A few days later the shed disappeared and she lived happily to the end of her life with the necklace.

Grace Allsobrook (9)
Trefonen School

A DAY IN THE LIFE OF EMILY AND SARAH!

Mountains
'Emily!' Sarah screamed. Emily woke up with a jump. Sarah was trapped in a mud pit (Emily's brown jumper) with a snake (Sarah's toy snake) strangling her. Emily flung off her PJs and flung on some clothes. She ran to Sarah's rescue. Emily wrestled the snake down to the floor, while Sarah climbed out of the mud pit, mud squelching everywhere.

They escaped from the scary snake and walked down the tall mountain. Sarah asked Emily where the food cabin was.
'I don't know!' exclaimed Emily. 'It might be round here.'
They searched everywhere, high and low, then a friendly mountain climber shouted, 'Breakfast is here!'
They ran in, pushing each other out of the way. They sat down at the table and started gobbling their food down.

The wolof
After breakfast, the girls decided to set off in search of the wolof. The wolof had a pointy nose with a weird, gruesome face, a little bit like Sarah and Emily's next-door neighbour's face.

Sarah followed Emily into the forest. 'Quick! A tiger! Into the cave!' screamed Sarah. Emily and Sarah ran into the cave to hide from the tiger. A few minutes later, the girls crept out of the cave.
'Look, there's a wolof,' whispered Emily.
They spotted a wolof feeding her baby. The cat-wolof stood up and walked away with her baby following.
'Where shall we go now?' asked Sarah.
Emily thought for a moment, 'Let's go to the sea!' exclaimed Emily.

Under the sea
'Glub, glub, glub,' giggled Sarah.
Emily laughed, then quickly stopped. 'Look!' hissed Emily. 'There's a catfish,' she pointed to the tabby cat who passed by. Emily gave a yelp.
'There's a shark,' she gulped.
Sarah took out her camera and click!

'Our brother would love this, wouldn't he?' Emily whispered. 'I'm getting a bit scared though. Can we go somewhere else now?'

Sarah grinned. 'Let's go to the dance studio,' she hollered.

In the dance studio

'And now introducing, Emily and Sarah,' announced Sarah.

They waltzed on stage, trying to look proud. Sarah tried to stand on tiptoes and twirl around, but she just fell over. Emily just stood there, waving her arms.

'Come on, do something, a purlet or a fincy fancy,' laughed Sarah.

Emily smiled, 'What about a binuet or a glempet?'

The girls collapsed in a heap of laughter.

'This is an inny winny,' grinned Emily.

She jumped up, stuck out her left arm and her right leg. She flapped her left arm and kicked with her right leg. As she did that, she nodded her head. Then she squeaked, 'Inny, domdom, winny, dee dee.'

Sarah laughed so much she fell over. After 2 minutes of watching Sarah laugh, Emily announced she was bored. 'Let's go to the fair,' she yelled.

At the fair

'I want to go on the roller coaster!' shouted Emily. She jumped into a small purple car with the number 2 on and she hung on to the handle. 'Wheee!' she shrieked. Sarah watched her.

After the girls had been on the dodgems, merry-go-round and the glider, and they had won something each on the wheel of prizes (a toy cat and a toy panda). Sarah announced that she wanted to go on the big slide.

'So do I,' agreed Emily.

They walked nervously over to the big slide. Now you may be thinking that Emily and Sarah must be big babies to pretend stuff like this, they are. They are both 4½.

The girls looked up at the slide. Emily counted how many rungs the ladder had. '5, 22, 3, 50, 76 . . .' It had more than 76. Sarah took up some courage and walked over to the bottom of the ladder. Emily followed.

'Come on then Emily,' gulped Sarah. 'We can do it.' They climbed up to the very top and stopped there. 'You go down first,' ordered Sarah. 'No way!' argued Emily.

'Coming through, big bully coming through.' The girls' big brother came up to the top of the slide. 'Bye girls!' he shouted. He gave Sarah a little push. Sarah bumped into Emily making both of the girls fall down the slide.

At the bottom Sarah whispered, 'I feel sick.'

Emily nodded. She felt sick as well. 'Where shall we go now?' asked Emily.

'To the theatre. No! The BBC! Even better CBBC!'

In the CBBC studios
'Hello, I'm Sarah Bell . . .'

'And I'm Emily Bell.'

'Today on the CBBC channel you will be watching Mona the Vampire, Tracy Beaker and non-stop madness. We are giving away prizes for any of you that phone up and sing the theme tune from you fave TV show.'

'Emily! Sarah! Dinner!' their mum shouted.

The girls waved goodbye and ran to eat their lunch.

Georgina Wilson (10)
Weston Lullingfields Primary School